THE PACIFIST

NEW WAVE NEWSROOM

JENNY HOLIDAY

new wave
newsroom

Edited by Gwen Hayes. Copyedited by Polly Watson. Cover design and formatting by Zack Taylor. Cover photo by ysbrand via Deposit Photos.

First edition October 25, 2016

ISBN: 978-0-9950927–4-7

For ZT.

CHAPTER ONE

August 1984

TONY

I wasn't supposed to be taking photographs this semester, but the picture practically composed itself.

It was the tail end of summer, and the courtyard was overripe, teeming with life. Large willow trees poured their lush green waterfalls down toward the lawn, which was studded with purple flowers.

The girl had her back to me, but I knew she was beautiful. There was something about her, her posture maybe, or just her aura, though I normally didn't go in for that kind of hippie shit. She wore a loose, slouchy, mustard-yellow dress belted at the waist with a wide black leather belt, and black ankle boots. She was tall, and her hair added another couple of inches of height, so she blocked my view of the guy she was with.

Still, it was obvious what they were doing. They were

locked in a close embrace, and the guy had his arms around her, holding her tight.

Even the animals were transfixed. Well, one of them, anyway. A single squirrel stood a few feet from the amorous couple, head cocked, staring at them, which wasn't necessarily saying much, because the squirrels on this campus were domesticated, fat, and demanding, stalking students who dared to eat outside in Allenhurst College's various quads and courtyards.

There was no doubt in my mind that Beth would run this shot, even though I technically wasn't on the newspaper staff anymore. She might even do it in color, despite the expense. Sometimes the *Allenhurst Examiner*'s first issue of the year—the welcome-back edition—ran a color front page. Getting a shot on the front of the first issue of the year would be a nice way to start what was, depressingly, year five of my degree. It turns out that when you spend more of your time at the newspaper office and partying than you do in class, it catches up with you. Which was why this semester was going to be about classes and nothing else. If I put my head down and worked hard, I could graduate in December. That meant no photography. No parties. No girls. But the idea of one more photo in the paper as a bookend of sorts, a coda to my career as the *Examiner*'s photographer? It had undeniable appeal.

Especially this particular photo.

Another squirrel sauntered over and joined the first, and I had to bite my tongue to keep from laughing. This shot was gonna be so perfect, people were going to think I'd staged it.

It almost felt too easy, inserting myself into this crystalline moment and making it mine. They were standing in the perfect location inside my viewfinder, about two-thirds of the way over from the edge of the ivy-covered building I was planning to use as a framing device. I wouldn't even have to get them to sign release forms, because neither of their faces showed—which was good, because although I wasn't above a little mischief in pursuit of the perfect shot, I didn't relish the idea of interrupting that heated kiss.

I lifted my camera and adjusted the focus. It was going to be an amazing shot, and though I would take the credit for it, it wouldn't be because of me. I was merely lucky enough to stumble onto a perfect scene that had already composed itself.

Click.

CHAPTER TWO

TONY

"Tony, there's someone here to see you."

It was Beth calling through the door of the darkroom, though I had already recognized her knock. Beth was the editor of the *Examiner* and though she was a relentless newshound, she had a surprisingly tentative knock, at least compared to Jenny, her predecessor. Funny that I'd spent so much time in this darkroom over the years that I could distinguish between the knocks of my editors.

I wasn't supposed to be here, working on the second issue of the year. I should have been in my apartment, getting a jump on my reading for the four classes I was taking this semester. I'd never successfully passed four classes in a semester before. If Jenny was still in charge, she would have kicked me out. Beth, who knew all about my self-imposed Semester of No Fun, had not. So, like a junkie in search of a fix, here I was, hunched over in the red-tinged darkness.

Beth's knock was joined by another, more insistent one. More of a pounding, really. Definitely someone else.

The door shook. I moved quickly to shove the photo paper into its black plastic bag, lest my more aggressive visitor knock the door off the hinges and flood the room with light.

"Give me a sec!" Who could want to see me so urgently? My twin sister, Tanya, had graduated, as had Jenny and Dawn and most of my close friends who would know to find me here. That was part of the point. No friends left on campus meant no social temptation and should have made it easier to put my head down and plow through Introduction to Geology. (Yes, I had failed Rocks for Jocks the first time around.)

The pounding continued. "Hang *on*!" I double-checked that my paper was secure in its bag before closing the bag in its box. Then I swung open the door, blinking against the sudden brightness.

Blinking against the sudden beauty.

Because it was her. The girl from the picture. And, all warm medium-brown skin, flashing brown eyes, and scarlet-painted lips, she was gorgeous.

She was also not pleased.

"What the hell is this?" she yelled, waving a copy of Tuesday's paper, which featured her courtyard kiss on the cover. The paper had an Overheard/Overseen on Campus section, and we sometimes ran a photo in it. Beth had, as I'd predicted, moved the feature to the front page and run my shot in color.

"Hey." I flashed my trademark grin that was so popular with the ladies. Even though I wasn't supposed to be deploying that grin this year, it might mitigate some of the tension rolling off this girl. "It's nice to properly meet you. I'm Tony."

I held out my hand for her to shake, but she looked at it like I was offering her a handful of shit. So I did a lame stretching/fixing-my-hair thing to cover the fact that my overture had been rebuffed, which was stupid, because as pretty as she was, what did I care what this girl thought of me? It was the Semester of No Fun, right?

"Well, Tony," she said, her voice having gone quiet, which was jarring after the yelling. It did something to me, hearing my name on her lips like that, all breathy and intimate. It made me comfortable and uncomfortable at the same time, which made no sense, but there it was. "How about we start with the fact that you have ruined my life."

Okay then. Though she'd turned down the volume, the anger was clearly still there, judging by the way she over-enunciated each syllable and glared at me with her hands on her hips.

"I'm sorry," Beth said. I swung my gaze to my editor. I'd forgotten she was there. "Did he not get you to sign a photo release?"

"I didn't need one," I told her. "No one's face was showing. The subjects can't be identified."

The angry girl let the newspaper flutter to the ground at my feet, dropping it like it was no longer worth the minimal effort required to keep holding it. "The subjects can't be identified?" she echoed, her eyebrows moving up, creating lines in her otherwise smooth forehead. "How many black girls with Afros are there on this campus, do you think?"

Aww, shit. I hadn't thought of it that way. "I don't know," I said, my mind spinning with the effort of trying to come up with an example of another Afro-sporting girl. But even if I could, her point was valid. Allenhurst was a pretty white place. Still, I wasn't sure what she was so worked up about. It was a great shot. One of my best ever. It would be given a place of pride in my portfolio, assuming I ever got my act together enough to graduate and *need* a portfolio. So, really, why did this girl have her undies in such a bunch? "You looked amazing in the shot, though," I said, deploying some flattery to bolster my case. "That dress was totally rad, and there was something about the way you were holding yourself, your posture, that was really compelling."

"My posture," she said, her nose wrinkling like she'd smelled something gross. "My posture was compelling. That's all you have to say?"

"What do you want me to say? You can't retract a photo."

"I want you to say, 'I'm sorry I ruined your life.' I want you to understand that you can't just walk around invading people's private moments without creating consequences for them."

Whoa. I held up my hands like she was robbing me. Melodramatic much?

She rolled her eyes, but really quickly and really subtly, so much so that I almost missed it. Most people would have, but I had trained myself to see things other people didn't. And for some reason, that low-key eye roll made me angrier than a more overt one would have. It was like I was so incredibly far beneath her that it wasn't even worth her time for her to properly communicate that sentiment to me.

Then she turned and started walking away.

So this girl nearly broke down my darkroom door and now she was *dismissing* me?

Yeah, no, not so much.

I let the jet of anger that erupted in my chest propel me after her. "Wait!" I shouted, ignoring Beth's attempts to call me back. The angry girl kept walking briskly. I followed her out of the warren that was the *Examiner*'s basement news-room. "Hang on!" I said, as she mounted the stairs that would take her back to the ground floor of the building. She ignored me. It was like I wasn't even there, and god*damn*, that made me mad. "So you just came to shake your finger at me and now you're not even going to speak to me?" I called as I finally caught up with her, trying not to pant.

That stopped her. She turned and paused, poised in the doorway, one foot inside the building, the other out. "What's left to say, Tony? You were actually right: you *can't* retract a photo."

Two things about what she said pissed me off. The first was that she knew my name, and I still didn't know hers. She had barged onto *my* turf. Why should she have the upper hand? The second was the way she said "can't," stressing it ever so slightly, like it was such a shock that someone as simple as I could be right about something. Her words were sharp little sticks poking at my gut.

"What's your name?" I asked. The question came out sounding mean, which I hadn't necessarily intended, but that was okay, because something about this girl had me spoiling for a fight.

"Why? So the next time you intrude on a private moment and plaster it all over the newspaper, you can add my name to the caption?" One side of her scarlet-painted upper lip curled, a little proto-sneer. Like with the eye roll, I was annoyed that I apparently wasn't worthy of a full-blown sneer.

"I'm not sure how you can say that was a private moment," I shot back. "If you wanted it to be private, maybe you shouldn't have been doing it, oh, I don't know, *in public*."

She surprised me then by sighing. Those lips I'd been staring at so intently fell open to make room for the long, resigned exhalation. That sigh confused me, because it felt like a defeated sigh, but surely that couldn't be right? I couldn't have won that easily? It also immediately brought to mind other circumstances in which lips could part on a sigh like that, but I shoved that thought right back down where it came from. The semester had barely even started, and no way was I so hard up that I was going to let myself perv on this prickly, unreasonable chick, no matter how gorgeous she was.

Then her eyes slipped closed and her shoulders slumped, confirming my initial sense that the fight had left her. That something had shifted between us. When she opened her eyes, her gaze held mine for a long moment before she turned again to leave.

If she had surprised me with that sigh, with how easily she'd given up the fight just then, I downright *shocked* myself by reaching my hand out, just before she escaped, and resting it on her arm. I wasn't exerting any pressure, but it was enough to stop her. "Tell me about these consequences," I said. But even as I posed the question, I asked myself why? Why did I care? I didn't owe this girl anything. All I had done was take a photo of her in a public place. Still, I needed to know. "Tell me about the consequences you mentioned." I tried not to think about how I was touching her bare skin, about how incredibly soft it was.

As if she'd heard the very thoughts I was trying not to have, she dropped her gaze to my hand on her arm. My own gaze followed, and I noticed for the first time that she was wearing a Siouxsie and the Banshees T-shirt. I added that fact to pile of surprises that had accumulated over the past few minutes. I loved that band. I wanted to tell her, but it was the wrong thing to say.

And then the touch seemed wrong, too. It was just my hand on her arm, and she hadn't objected or moved to escape it, but it was suddenly intrusive, too intimate—like the picture? Shit. Had she been right about that?

Maybe it was just that it was too much to adjust to, this moment of peace, of human contact, after our adversarial introduction. Too whiplash-inducing.

"I should not have been kissing that guy," she said, still looking at my hand.

"He wasn't identifiable." I'm not sure if I intended to reassure her or to defend myself. Regardless, from my angle, she'd been completely obscuring her paramour in the shot. All you could see of him were his arms wrapped around her, and he hadn't been wearing a watch or anything else that might have given him away. "You couldn't tell who he was."

"Yes," she said, finally lifting her gaze and looking me in the eye. "But you could tell who he *wasn't*." Then she shook my hand off her arm and jogged down the steps that ran from the door to the sidewalk. I'd been dismissed. Again.

I *really* didn't like being dismissed by this girl, apparently. "Hey!" I called after her, loud enough for her to stop at the bottom of the steps and shoot me a skeptical look, like she was a mature-beyond-her-years person tolerating the whim of a child. "Tell me your name."

"My name is…" She paused long enough that I suspected she was making something up, giving me a fake name. "My name is Laraline."

LARALINE

So far, the Semester of Fun was not turning out to be very much fun.

I mean, kissing Brian had been fun, but certainly not enough that it had been worth the trouble it had caused… and had yet to cause. I still had dinner with my parents to get through on Friday.

I let myself into my apartment and blew out a breath. Wow, that Tony guy had rattled me. I don't know what I had expected. That he would be contrite, I guess. It hadn't occurred to me that the person who took such an amazing picture—and it *had* been amazing—would be capable of being such a shithead.

"Dove? Hey!"

My roommate, Cynthia, emerged from the kitchen into the small entryway of our apartment, wiping her hands on her apron.

"My name is Laraline," I said, for the second time today.

"Right," she said. "Sorry. I keep forgetting."

I was in the process of trying to shed my nickname, Dove. The peacemaker. *Laraline* was Latin for "seagull," and at some point early in my undergrad career, my friends had decided that I was misnamed. If I was going to be a bird, they said, I should be the bird of peace, since I spent as much time keeping the peace in my family as I did studying. My campaign of appeasement had begun ten years ago when my sister, Phoebe, got sick, and it had intensified when she died. It was like since the transplant didn't work, I had moved into overcompensation mode, constantly trying to make things okay, even though the rational part of my brain knew that was impossible.

So: Dove. It started as a joke, and then it just kind of… stuck. No more, though. It was the Semester of Fun, so I'd forced Dove to fly south.

But if you had to explicitly label a thing—it's the Semester of Fun!—and keep reminding yourself of the existence of that thing, it probably meant that thing wasn't going to come naturally to you.

Which is another way of saying that the Semester of Fun had been Jason's idea.

Not that label, and not necessarily my interpretation of it, which was that I was going to go out there and kiss a bunch of other boys. I had a feeling he wouldn't like that part. Like a lot of men, Jason was blind to his own double standards. He was my father's protégé in more ways than one.

He'd sat me down on his last visit, just before school started, and said that he would be back at Christmas and would want to "talk seriously" to me then, but that we shouldn't be "exclusive" for this "last little stretch," you know, "just to make sure." We'd been together so long, we should experience the world without each other for a few months, he'd said.

I was surprised by how much he'd hurt my feelings. I'd long since resigned myself to the fact that Jason wasn't going to be the great love of my life in the style of the movies. We would never kiss in the rain or fight duels to defend each other's honor. I wasn't even convinced that kind of love existed. But I liked Jason a lot. He understood the way things were in my family, and that wasn't nothing.

And there was so much invested in the idea of Jason and me.

So when he'd gotten on that plane to go back to Greece, leaving me hollowed out by betrayal, I'd decided hell, maybe he had a point. I didn't *feel* like he had a point, but my rational mind, the part that was apparently in charge of my pride, forced me to have a "what's good for the goose is good for the gander" response.

And though it had begun with me merely going through the motions, I had started to actually…have fun. At least until that photo ran in the paper. Flirting was fun. Kissing was fun. As the first week of my last year of grad school unfolded, I started to *really* feel it. It was dawning on me that this semester was really it. My last chance to do what I wanted every day.

My last chance to be my own person.

My last chance to…live.

Maybe Jason had been onto something.

"You had some calls." Cynthia pulled me out of my thoughts and into a quick, hard half-hug. "Come into the kitchen. I'm making cookies for work. I need a tester."

"I'm sorry I jumped down your throat with the name thing." A rush of affection for my best friend inspired me to grab her and give her a proper, full-on hug. We'd been assigned as roommates five years ago, our freshman year. The dormitory gods had been smiling on me the day they hitched me to the wide-eyed farm girl from Iowa. I hadn't thought so at the time, because we seemed to have nothing in common. She was a blue-eyed, blond-haired daughter of corn farmers, at Allenhurst on a scholarship and majoring in civil engineering. I was a black girl from Boston's Beacon Hill, majoring in art history, and I was a legacy at the school. Not only had my father attended, he was a famous professor in the classics department. As a faculty kid, I received free tuition, even though we had more than enough to cover it. Once Cynthia and I got over the shock of our differences and discovered that your sameness with another person could be much bigger than your difference, I had often wished that I could somehow transfer my tuition waiver to her.

"It's okay," she said, pulling away but keeping hold of my hand and leading me into the kitchen.

"What kind this time?" I asked, inhaling the heavenly smell of caramelized sugar.

"Chocolate chip with crunched-up potato chips."

I laughed but snagged one, knowing the weird combo would be amazing. Maybe it was the engineer in her, but Cynthia loved tinkering in the kitchen, and coming up with cookie creations that were as delicious as they were unlikely was one of her trademarks.

"Oh my God," I said through a mouthful of the sweet-salty goodness. "The jerks at work don't deserve these. Can I bring some to the rally tomorrow night?"

"Oh, right, that's tomorrow! Yes, of course." She started rummaging in a cupboard for a cookie tin. "Let's take them all. Much better cause than Rogers and Steenburger." Cynthia worked in an administrative capacity at a small engineering firm in the next town over. She had hoped it would be a foot in the door to an actual engineering job. It irritated the hell out of me that a year and a half later, she was still answering the phones and doing grunt-work to support the guys who worked there.

And making them cookies. Which was why I was always trying to steal them. Rogers and Steenburger and their minions didn't deserve her cookies.

Cynthia went to the phone mounted on the wall and picked up a piece of notepaper she'd tacked to the bulletin board beneath it. "So, your mom called twice, once at five and again at five-thirty. She wants you to call her back before eight."

Which translated into: she wanted me to call her back

before my father got home. "I'm seeing them tomorrow night, but I suspect she wants to 'strategize' on how to handle my father after Photogate."

Which translated into: after a speech about how shocked and disappointed she was, she would feed me the lines that would placate my father. Because that's how we rolled in our family, post-Phoebe.

I had hoped against hope that my father wouldn't see Tuesday's newspaper. That he'd be busy getting the new semester off the ground. In addition to his usual undergrads, he had two new doctoral students starting this fall—people came from all over the world to work with my dad because he was the world's foremost expert on the architecture of ancient Greece.

But no. Tuesday evening he had made a rare appearance at my apartment. Though he would often pick me up outside when I was heading home for a visit, he hadn't been upstairs since the day Cynthia and I moved in four years ago.

To say he'd been angry was an understatement. He didn't blow up, though, which was actually worse than if he had. He'd merely informed me that he'd be picking me up Friday at five and taking me back to Boston for dinner.

"Annnndd," Cynthia drawled, hugging the notepaper to her chest, "you had *one* more message."

"Who was it?" I asked, wondering why she was being so coy.

"Brian."

Aww, crap. See? This was why the Semester of Fun was not all it was cracked up to be. Brian had been nice enough. He was an art history undergrad, and he was cute. We'd been at a guest lecture on Cubism and had gotten into a bit of a debate afterward. When he'd asked me to go for a drink, I'd thought, *Well, what the hell? Semester of Fun, right?*

"Who's Brian?" Cynthia asked. "Is he the guy you were kissing in that picture?" She had seen the picture, of course —the whole campus had seen the picture—but I'd been steadfast in my refusal to discuss it with her, which wasn't typical. Usually we talked everything to death.

"He's no one."

"No one who called here and, when I told him you weren't home, asked me what your favorite kind of flower was?" she prodded, eyebrows raised. "He *was* the picture guy!"

I sighed. I really, really didn't want Brian to become a thing. He was supposed to have been a kiss, and that was it.

Cynthia tried to hand me the notepaper, but I waved her off. "I'm not calling him back." I moved to take a cookie from the cooling rack, but she pivoted and blocked me.

"But who *is* he?"

"You know what Jason said before he left," I protested, hating that I was suddenly on the defensive. "I wasn't doing anything wrong."

She didn't speak right away, just stared at me with her eyes narrowed for what felt like an hour. Then she finally said, "Listen." She was speaking in her Engineer Voice, the one she used when she was really applying herself to a problem. "I don't care about Jason. I've never said this to you in so many words, but I'm going to say it now: You don't have to marry Jason."

Her words were a slap to the face. I actually reared back a little, physically. But when I opened my mouth to protest that yes, I did have to marry Jason, that I even *wanted* to marry Jason, or at least I *didn't mind* marrying Jason, all things considered, she presented me with her palm.

But then, inexplicably, she lightened up and flashed me a smile. "I also don't care if you dropped trou on the quad and participated in an orgy. I just want to know who this Brian guy is! You've been dating Jason the entire time I've known you, and suddenly here's this other guy? Come on! Give me something!"

I laughed, partly because the exaggerated faces she was making were funny, but partly because of the weird emotional roller coaster I'd been on today, and gave up my stonewalling. "He's just this art history kid—a sophomore. He isn't a big deal. Honestly. If he was a big deal, I would tell you."

"A younger man. About time." She was referring to the fact that Jason was five years older than I was. She handed me a cookie.

What was I going to do next year when I didn't have Cynthia around to make cookies for me? Well, that and coax out all my secrets? The prospect of Cynthia just...not being there made my throat tighten.

"Hey," I said, suddenly thinking that the Semester of Fun didn't just have to be about boys. "A band I'm kind of interested in is playing at the A-Hole tonight. You want to check them out?" Since I'd started grad school and Cynthia had started working full-time, we didn't hang out the way we used to. Of course, we saw each other all the time in the apartment, but a show on a "school night" wasn't something we would generally do these days.

My roommate grinned. "I sure do."

CHAPTER THREE

TONY

The band sucked.

I shouldn't have been surprised. It wasn't like a *decent* band would be playing the Allenhurst Tap Room, aka the A-Hole, aka the cheapest of the cheap campus bars. Still, I'd heard good things about them—they were an up-and-coming band out of Portland, Maine. I'd killed myself getting my studying done so I could justify coming out of my cage for a couple hours to hear them, so it was disappointing that they hadn't been worth my effort. I would have had more fun staying home and watching *Dynasty*, and I hated *Dynasty*. My sister used to make me watch it with her in our years together on campus, and though I was not a fan of the show, I *was* a fan of my sister, and the show made me think of her.

Well, still. I was up-to-date with my homework, which was an extremely strange feeling, and I was already out. Maybe I'd call Beth and some of the newspaper people and try to get them to come meet me for a drink.

I made my way to the hallway back by the restrooms, digging in my pocket for a dime.

There was someone already talking on the pay phone.

This is the part where, if this were a movie, I wouldn't recognize her. The ingredients were there for me not to recognize her. Her back was to me, and she was wearing a fedora, so her hair was mostly obscured.

But, yeah, I would recognize Laraline anywhere. I was only surprised that I hadn't ever noticed her before. Campus was big, but not *that* big, and Laraline was unambiguously gorgeous. After she'd stormed off the other day, I'd asked around the newspaper office—reporters are nothing if not well-connected—and found out she was an art history grad student. And that she hadn't given me a fake name, which had been unaccountably satisfying.

I wished I had my camera. I usually took it with me everywhere, but since I was breaking a rule by going out, I'd decided not to break a second by bringing my camera. Bringing my camera would lead to picture-taking, which would lead to time in the darkroom, which was decidedly not where I was supposed to be spending this semester.

But I suddenly had this vision of a series of photographs of Laraline from behind. I had the courtyard kiss. I had her now. She had changed out of the Siouxsie shirt and was wearing a purple dress that was belted at the waist with the same wide black belt I'd seen on her in the courtyard. And the hat. It was beige, with a purple band that matched the dress. It brought to mind Indiana Jones. You know, if Indiana Jones was wearing a dress that showed off the flare of his hips to perfection and then stopped mid-thigh, show-casing a pair of long, slim legs.

But, yeah, it was the Semester of No Fun, so I wasn't going there.

There was also the fact that this chick hated me.

So I shoved down the inconvenient surge of attraction, tapped her on the shoulder, and said, "Are you almost done?"

LARALINE

Are you *kidding* me?

Between my undergrad and my master's studies, I'd been at Allenhurst for going on six years, and I'd never once laid eyes on this Tony guy. And now I'd seen him twice in one day? It was theoretically possible that he was a freshman, but there was just no way. To begin with, I didn't think an eighteen-year-old would have that kind of beard. Tony was rocking a serious five-o'clock shadow. I wasn't normally into the raggedy look—Jason was always impeccably clean-shaven—but it worked for Tony. And would he have been so comfortably ensconced in the darkroom at the college newspaper if he had been brand-new to campus? There was a kind of entitlement about Tony that said that he was comfortable in his surroundings. Maybe that was just him, though. He had talked about my posture, but *he* carried himself with a kind of grace that was…hard to look away from.

But, whoa, it might be the Semester of Fun, but I did have standards. So when he said, "Are you almost done?" I just curled my lip slightly and turned my back to him. But then I was stuck, because I didn't want him to know that I was talking to *my mother*. God. The band had been so bad, and I'd suddenly realized that I'd forgotten to call her back. And, well, let's just say that calling her back at 9:45 p.m. from a pay phone at a bar, as subpar an option as that was, was infinitely preferable to not calling her back at all.

Even though I curled myself into the tightest ball I could and put my hand over my mouth and the receiver, I could *feel* him there, hovering, watching me. And I knew, somehow, that no matter how long I talked, he would not go away. His attention should have been unwelcome. But I couldn't stop thinking about that damned stubble. What would it feel like to touch with my fingers? What would it feel like against my cheek?

My skin started to prickle, and I was having trouble focusing on my mother, who was talking about the fact that Jason and my father were working on a new paper together, and how important that was. Jason needed to publish in quality journals during his postdoctoral fellowship if he wanted to get a tenure-track professorship. My father was giving up so much to help his former PhD student. Et cetera, et cetera. I was tempted to ask what all that had to do with me, but I knew the answer. We needed to be quiet and let the men do their important work. We needed to support them, not kiss boys with inexplicably attractive five-o'clock shadows.

Wait. That wasn't right. Brian didn't have a five-o'clock shadow.

Tony coughed, and my face burned.

I couldn't be here anymore. I had to fly away before Tony immobilized me, like an insect pinned to a board. So I cut off my mother, whispering, "I'm sorry, but I have to go. We'll talk more tomorrow night." I didn't wait for her expression of shock; I just hung up.

Before I turned to relinquish the phone to Tony, I arranged my face into a mask that I hoped communicated annoyance, but not too much of it. I didn't want him thinking he'd rattled me.

But, oh man, when I turned, I might as well have been that insect, except I didn't need him to stick a pin in me—apparently I was just going to sacrifice myself. All I could do was stand there and stare at him and hope that my mouth stayed closed. I'd seen him before, when I'd turned after he tapped my shoulder, but only for an instant. Tony's hair was dark brown and kind of long-ish, chin length. He reminded me of a darker River Phoenix. Earlier today, his hair had been loose, flopping around his ears. But he'd done some kind of pompadour thing with it this evening, so it was puffed up and slicked back off his pale face. He was wearing glasses, too, which also hadn't been there earlier. They were horn-rimmed glasses with black frames, like you'd associate with the 1950s. They should have been geeky, but they looked good. There was a kind of Gothy nerd-chic air about him that was, well... It worked for him.

We stood there staring at each other, neither of us moving until he lifted the beer he was holding and took a long pull. The action drew my attention to his lips, which were pinker than a boy's lips should be allowed to be, wrapped around the neck of the bottle, and to his Adam's apple, which moved up and down as he swallowed. He had tipped his head back only slightly, so he was able to keep looking at me while he drank. I found myself swallowing in concert with him, licking my suddenly dry lips.

Were we having some kind of standoff? Why did I feel like breaking eye contact first would amount to a sort of surrender?

And, more importantly, why did I care?

I didn't. So I moved to get past him, but the hallway around the phone was narrow, and since I didn't wait for him to adjust his position, we brushed against each other. Like, my *boobs* brushed against his chest. I was mortified when my nipples reacted instantly, turning into hard, aching peaks.

He smiled as if he knew what was happening, though of course that wasn't possible—thank God.

After I'd successfully pushed past him, he said, "Good night, Laraline."

I didn't look back.

CHAPTER FOUR

LARALINE

I wasn't sure Take Back the Night was really my thing. I mean, I absolutely believed in the cause. It was impossible not to be moved as women shared their stories, passed a flame from candle to candle, and spoke about how the night should belong to everyone, how we should all be able to walk without fear. And when my friend Danielle, the rally's organizer, had invited me, of course I'd said yes.

But I'd started thinking, after I saw my picture in the paper, that in addition to this semester being my last chance to have a little fun, it was also my last chance to do anything meaningful. Jason would come visit in December, we'd have our "serious discussion," and then, after graduation in the spring, I'd take my MA in art history and stuff it in a drawer. I would become Mrs. Jason Williams, exchanging my father's name for my husband's.

And I'd never done anything important in my life, not really.

I'd been thinking that maybe I should. It sounded

impossibly naïve, but maybe in addition to being the girl who kissed boys, I could also try, for the next few months, to be the girl who…helped. I couldn't organize rallies like Danielle—I wasn't a charismatic leader type—which is why I was thinking that Take Back the Night wasn't precisely my cup of tea.

I wanted to do more than stand around and hold a candle and shout, anyway. I wanted to look back and be able to say that I made a measurable if tiny difference in the world. That way, later, when I was living my mom's life, typing Jason's notes and throwing parties for his colleagues, I would be able to look back and say, "I did this one thing."

I just couldn't figure out what that "thing" should be.

"This is Kari," Danielle shouted into a microphone at the top of the student center staircase, startling me from my thoughts. "It's getting dark, so I don't know if you can see Kari's face." She clicked on a flashlight, then lowered her voice to say to Kari, "Close your eyes, sweetie."

I, along with the crowd, gasped at the black eye marring Kari's otherwise pale complexion.

"Kari asked me to tell you that her ex-boyfriend did this."

I had to look away. I had no firsthand experience with that kind of thing. It was definitely safe to characterize my father as a forceful man. Maybe even an angry one, at least since Phoebe died. He got his way, but he did it via a different kind of power. I'd never seen him raise a hand to my mother or anyone else. He didn't need to.

I scanned the crowd. Because I'd come early to help Danielle set up, I was perched a few steps below where she and Kari and the other speakers stood, so I had a good view of the assembly. The turnout was decent for the first week of school—maybe three hundred people, mostly women but a few men.

And one of those men was a photographer.

Tony. There was no mistaking the camera-wielding guy in the ripped black T-shirt, torn jeans, and leather wrist cuffs.

A hot jet of rage erupted up my spine. Who did he think he was? The way he just walked around like he expected the world to display itself to him, to showcase its private, vulnerable moments… The entitlement was breathtaking.

"Kari wants to say a few words." Danielle handed off the mic and moved down a step.

She was only one step above me now, so I grabbed her arm and pulled her ear down to my mouth. "There's a creep photographer out there. I'm going to go run him off."

She followed my gaze. "Are you kidding? We should be giving him an all-access pass. Media coverage is exactly what we need to spread our message." I hadn't thought of it that way, but, duh, of course she was right. "I wonder if he's just a guy taking pictures or if he's here from a newspaper or something," she went on.

"I think he's with the campus paper," I said, keeping my eyes on Mr. Gothy River Phoenix as he weaved in and out of the throng, taking pictures of the crowd. Tall and skinny, he had a lanky grace and seemed utterly focused on his mission. I'd been thinking of him before as entitled, but maybe *entitled* wasn't the right word, exactly. Maybe it was more like *determined. Persevering.*

"Even better. I'd really like to get him to take a portrait of Kari afterward." Danielle looked at her watch and back at Kari, who was wrapping up her speech. "Shit, though. I gotta go back on." She shot a longing glance toward Tony.

I sighed. "I'll go talk to him."

"You will?" Danielle beamed at me.

"Yeah. He owes me."

TONY

Everyone thought I was such a slacker. I looked the type, I guess. I wasn't a full-on Goth—I wasn't hitting the clubs on the weekends with teardrops painted on my face or anything —but my naturally dark hair, my preference for moody music, and my tendency to hang around in the darkroom fussing over my art sent a certain message, I guess. And, to be fair, my shitty grades kind of ratified my slacker status.

But I was a selective slacker. I'd blow off class for a morning spent roaming campus with my camera, but that was its own kind of work. It took its own kind of dedication. Something happened to me when I was looking at the world through my viewfinder. I wasn't just concentrating—I entered another state of being. It was hard to explain, but the world sort of flattened itself out, went slightly mono-chromatic—which sounded like a bad thing but wasn't. It was what made pictures pop. Like, I could scan the scene and suddenly, a picture would resolve itself. Usually not all at once, but gradually. I'd be scanning, and I'd get a hint of something, a whisper that would make me stop and look closer, focus deeper, waiting until what was trying to come through was close enough to the surface that I could reach through my camera and get it.

It was addictive. It was why I'd failed Intro to Geology. And Elections in the Twentieth Century. And Democratic Theory.

It was proving hard to give up my camera this semester. Impossible, really.

As evidenced by the fact that here I was, prowling around a rally I wasn't covering for the newspaper.

Pop.

Pictures *usually* emerged gradually, playing tug-of-war with me as I teased them out of their surroundings. But with this girl, it was different. Apparently.

She just popped into my vision. Like that shot of her in the courtyard. Then, later, at the pay phone at the A-Hole: that shot, even though I hadn't had a camera with me to actually take it, had also arrived in my vision fully formed.

And now she was threading her way through the crowd toward me.

I watched her through my viewfinder, following her as she moved around clumps of people. I didn't even attempt to keep her in focus, just followed her, trying to keep her centered in the tiny window of glass between us.

My heart started to beat harder as she came closer. Which was dumb. What was she going to do? Sneer? Yell at me again? I'd been yelled at and worse in the line of duty, and it never fazed me. I'd do pretty much anything to get a picture. So I wasn't sure why the prospect of more of this girl's disdain was so off-putting.

I wanted to press the shutter-release button, and almost did about a hundred times as she got closer. I wouldn't use a flash, so her face would be in shadows, given the diminishing light, but she'd be sharply silhouetted against the midnight-blue sky that was on the verge of turning black.

She would be stunning.

But something stopped me. Maybe it was her indignation from before, her insistence that I'd overstepped a boundary by photographing her in the courtyard. Or the way she held herself apart. Maybe that's what my stupid babbling about her posture had been. She had a way of being in a crowd but not of it.

In other words: she popped.

So I just kept standing there stupidly until she was right in front of me, until, because I had the wrong lens on for a close-up, all I could see in my viewfinder was a blurry brown blob.

She had to reach out and physically touch my camera to get me to lower it. I refrained from pointing out that no one touched my camera. Ever. I didn't allow it. To begin with, the Leica had cost me more than a semester's tuition, even with the big discount I got from the camera store where I worked. But it was more than that. The camera was *mine*. It was an extension of me.

"Laraline," I said.

"Tony," she said back, her voice completely devoid of emotion. "Fancy meeting you here."

She was wearing a baggy pink T-shirt, peg-legged jeans with zippers at the ankles, and black Chuck Taylors that, I noticed with amusement, matched mine.

"I need you to do me a favor." She put her hands on her hips and squinted at me like I was a puzzle she was trying to figure out.

"Okay," I said immediately, and just as immediately regretted it. I didn't even know what she wanted. And I didn't owe her anything.

"You saw that girl Kari up there who was speaking?"

"Yeah."

"Maybe you couldn't see from back here, but she had a hell of a black eye."

"I did see. I was using a zoom lens." I started to say something else, because I was overcome with the impulse to apologize. But what for? I hadn't hurt Kari, and though I kind of felt like maybe I should apologize on behalf of all mankind, I didn't want to come off as the kind of egomaniac who would presume to speak for everyone. And, really, I'd already established myself in Laraline's eyes as the kind of person who didn't apologize, and I wasn't sure how to climb down from that stance now.

"Would you stick around afterward and take some portraits of her?"

Of course I would. The photographer in me didn't hesitate. The images would be arresting. But, as Jenny, my first editor, had taught me, you either took a picture because it was art, or you took a picture because it told a story. And a story needed a couple of things: a reason to be told, and a place to tell it.

Also, I was on hiatus. The Semester of No Fun and all that.

"I don't really take pictures anymore."

The puzzled look intensified. "Which is why you're out here with your camera?"

"Well…what would these portraits be for?"

"I'm not sure." She turned to look at the woman speaking, who seemed to be acting as emcee. "Do you work for the school paper?"

"No."

"Which is why I found you there in the darkroom earlier?"

God. I was making myself look like an idiot. "I used to. I helped out with the first couple of issues, but I'm taking a break this semester. I really need to concentrate on my studies."

She didn't say anything for a long time. The twilight had tipped over into full night, and candles burned around us, painting everything in a warm glow.

"Will you do it because I'm asking you to?"

"Yes," I said, because there really was no other answer. "Yes, I will."

LARALINE

The impromptu photography session inside the student center was uncomfortable for everyone. Well, maybe for everyone except Tony.

Kari was game. I didn't know her, had no idea where Danielle had found her, but it seemed like she'd recently left her boyfriend—no surprise there—and though she didn't want to be in the campus paper, she'd agreed to a portrait that Danielle would use at future rallies and fund-raisers. But being game didn't mean she wasn't nervous.

"My name isn't going to be on this, right?"

"Not at all," Danielle said quickly as Tony tested his flash.

There wasn't much that made Danielle uneasy, but the way she was kind of shifting from side to side was a tell. I got it. It's disquieting to be faced so viscerally with some-one's victimhood.

The only one who didn't seem bothered was Tony, which wasn't to say that he was glib or came off as uncaring. It was more that he was completely at ease, not at all awkward. He was clearly a good photographer. I mean, I knew he was a good photographer. But beyond that, he had great bedside manner. Kari couldn't have been at ease in a situation like this, but he was treating her with respect, asking her to move her chin "a hair to the right" and stuff, rather than moving it for her, which would have been the more efficient thing to do.

"You know what would be amazing?" Danielle exclaimed, drawing everyone's attention. "You know that thing where the board of governors is going to study the school's sexual assault policy this year and possibly revise it?"

I had heard a little bit about that. There had been two rape scandals on campus a couple years ago, and the administration had taken some heat for the way they handled the internal investigations. But the others must not have heard about it, because both Kari and Tony shook their heads.

"Okay, well, long story short," Danielle said, "is that the administration bungled a couple cases of sexual assault. It didn't act fast enough—or at all, really—in response to complaints. Dragged the complainants through the mud, that sort of thing. One of the things our group has been planning is to lobby the board of governors to encourage them to adopt a new, more stringent policy. We're going to launch a letter-writing campaign."

That was it. As soon as I heard it, I knew that this was my "thing." It was tangible. It would make a difference. I wasn't the type to shout through megaphones, but I could write letters.

"So I was thinking," Danielle went on, while I had my little revelation, "if you're okay with it, Kari, we could use your image for a promo blitz. We could launch a campaign."

"Posters and stuff would do a lot to raise awareness on campus," I said, seeing where she was going with this. I could put up posters.

"No way," Kari said. "I'm willing to help in, you know, a general way, but I don't want to be the cover girl for assault. It's one thing if you're going to use this on a poster at a rally where a limited and sympathetic audience sees it, but if my face is plastered all over campus, even without my name attached to the image, it's going to get around that it's me."

"Not necessarily," said Tony, who'd been quietly watching the conversation until that point. "I can't do it here —the light sucks—but I could photograph you in such a way that you wouldn't be identifiable."

"How would you manage that?" Danielle asked. "You have to see her face to see the black eye."

"If we do a close enough shot, you'll get the idea without seeing enough of her face to ID her," said Tony, looking, for some reason, at me. "I work at a camera shop. I can borrow lights and a seamless backdrop. It's a much better setup than this anyway, even if you just want a normal portrait like we originally talked about. The image will be much better."

"If I agreed to this," Kari said, "would I get to see the pictures before you did anything with them?"

She was talking to Danielle, who nodded. "We won't do anything unless you're okay with it." But then she turned to Tony. "I can't pay you. We have no budget."

"That's okay."

Danielle frowned. She was inherently skeptical. Of course, she'd only been a kid a decade ago during the bra burnings of the 1970s, but she wasn't that far removed from everyone's stereotype of the militant, man-hating feminist. "No offense or anything, but why would you do this for us?"

"I'm not doing it for you," Tony said, glancing at me. "I'm doing it for Laraline."

"Well, why would you do it for her?" Danielle countered, her frown deepening.

"Let's just say I owe her one."

CHAPTER FIVE

TONY

I was definitely quitting photography. And girls.

Just as soon as I got done taking pictures for the three of them that were currently perched on the end of the bed at my place, sipping Tabs while I set up lights.

The fact that I kept Tab at my apartment probably didn't bode well for my vow to quit dating. In my defense, it was old Tab. I hadn't had a thing with a girl since June, when I'd had a brief fling with a customer I'd met at the shop when she came in for a passport photo. But now she was back-packing through Europe, and I was off girls.

My sister was always accusing me of being "a stealth player." I didn't look the part, she said, given that I wasn't a jock or a prepster, but she claimed I used my sensitive, Gothy image to lure them in.

It *was* true that I had dated a lot of girls in my time at Allenhurst, but it was nothing so calculated. I *liked* girls. I liked them a lot. They were pretty, they smelled good, and they were generally easier to be around than guys. Even my closest platonic friends, like my former newspaper comrades Jenny and Dawn, were girls.

And I cared about girls, even if I'd never met one I wanted to be tied down to long-term. I cared about their comfort. So I stocked Tab and had a really comfy queen-size bed in my otherwise spartan studio apartment. So if that was the definition of a "stealth player," I'd own up to it.

"So I picked up a few different hats," I said to them, when I'd readied the small corner of my apartment I had turned into a makeshift studio. I laid them out on the kitchen table and spoke to Kari. "Seeing as you have auburn hair, I'm thinking we'll want to conceal it. The color is unique enough that it might make you recognizable to some people."

Laraline coughed. Hard. When I turned to her, she was giving me a super-annoyed look. Well. What could I say? I had learned my lesson when it came to unique hair.

The shoot went well after that. I tried to make it quick, as I assumed Kari wouldn't want to hang around being shot from a million different angles. "So we're good, I think," I said after twenty minutes. "I'll process these and be in touch." I looked between Danielle and Laraline. "Who should I call?"

"Me," Laraline said right away, inexplicably causing pleasure to pool in my stomach.

Danielle smiled. "Dove has agreed to spearhead the board of governors project," she said.

"Dove?" I asked, confused.

"Sorry. I meant Laraline," Danielle said at the same time that Laraline said, "It's an old nickname."

"Okay," I said, "hang back, and I'll get your number and we can talk a little about how you see these images being used. There are some effects I can create in the darkroom if you want." I generally didn't take advice on anything to do with photography, but damned if I didn't want her to stay.

When we'd seen the other two out, I went to the fridge and got her another Tab. "Unless you'd rather have a beer?" I asked.

"I wish, but I'd better not."

"Operating heavy machinery later?" I teased, popping open the soda and handing it to her.

"If only. Dinner with my parents, and I'm going to need my wits about me."

There wasn't a lot of seating in my place. It was basically a glorified dorm room with a kitchenette. I could have had more space if I'd been willing to have a roommate and share expenses, but I liked being on my own. I liked being able to putter around with my camera or walk around naked or whatever.

But living in such a small space didn't make for easy entertaining. Laraline sat on the edge of my bed, which, though I'd shoved it into a corner for the shoot, still took up most of the space. I didn't want her to think I was hitting on her—I knew somehow that that would send her flying. I needed to keep things light. So I pulled up one of my two kitchen chairs, which were the only other seating in the apartment.

"How come you need your wits about you for dinner with your parents?" I asked, trying not to stare at her bright red lips.

"Because they saw that picture you took of me kissing the wrong guy."

Well, shit. I had not seen that coming. "Why was he the wrong guy?" I really wanted to know. But, I reminded myself, I was keeping things light. "Have they pledged your troth to the prince of an adjacent kingdom so as to consolidate their power?"

She looked at me for a long time, long enough that I was pretty sure that was the end of our conversation, but then she said, "Something like that."

"Whoa!" Like, seriously: *whoa!* "I was just kidding."

She didn't smile. She didn't do anything but look off into space, making me think once again that we were done talking, that she would remember she hated me and that would be that. But she wasn't done surprising me yet.

"I'm supposed to marry this guy named Jason after I finish my degree. Jason is taller than I am, and he's black, too, so that was clearly not Jason in the picture you took. You could tell from the hands."

"I'm sorry." That I was apologizing surprised me, but it had just popped out. I mean, I *was* sorry, now that I'd heard about the "consequences" I'd created for her, but apologies weren't generally my thing. And despite everything, I *didn't* regret that photo.

She let her head fall back and huffed a sigh. "No, you were right. I *shouldn't* have been doing that in public if I didn't want to be seen." Her voice had gotten soft, and kind of small.

So I attempted once again to lighten the mood. I didn't do apologies, but I *did* know how to tease a girl. "Laraline, are we having a cease-fire?" I mimed laying down a weapon with a silly, dramatic flourish.

I got the smile I'd been fishing for. She raised her head and flashed it right at me. "I guess we are."

"What are you studying?" I asked, wanting to keep the détente going but trying to figure out a way to get to a place where I could ask the question that was clanging around inside my brain like an inmate bent on a prison break: *Who is Jason?*

"I'm doing an MA in art history," she said. "It's my last year. I'm writing my thesis now. I'm on track to defend it and graduate in May."

Tanya would laugh so hard at the idea that I was entertaining a grad student in my apartment. She was always accusing me of having a thing for older women. It wasn't a policy or anything, but there was some truth to it. When I was a freshman, I'd gone out for a couple months with a junior who was a fellow political science major. The relationship hadn't lasted, but after that, more often than not, when I dated, it was upperclassmen. Maybe it was a stereotype, but it seemed to me that older girls were more confident, less…tender. I'd jokingly told Tanya, who didn't believe I'd be able to pass my courses this term, that since I was a fifth-year undergrad, there would be no older women for me to date, and hence no distraction.

Obviously I hadn't counted on Laraline.

Laraline, who was *engaged*, it seemed. So her age really wasn't relevant.

"So that picture I took basically shows you cheating on your fiancé," I said, to myself as much as to her. To remind myself that there was a line, and that it needed toeing.

"My fiancé…" she said, like she was testing the word. "I guess so."

"You guess so?" I echoed. "Didn't you just say you were going to marry him after graduation?"

One corner of her mouth turned up. "It's kind of hard to explain."

I raised my eyebrows. "You sure you don't want that beer?"

She looked at me for a long moment before giving in to

the smile that had been threatening. "Yeah, actually, I would love a beer."

I took my time getting her a Blatz from the fridge. I needed to pull myself together here. I wasn't sure why this was all so unsettling, Maybe it was just that I'd never met anyone near my age who was married or imminently planning to be. But, I reminded myself, that was what most people did after college, right?

When I reemerged into the main room of the apartment and handed her the drink, she said, "I guess it's kind of like an arranged marriage. That sounds dumb, I know. Like, what century are we living in? And that's not really right. Jason is…my boyfriend. Kind of. Well, not this semester. But…" As she trailed off, she rolled her eyes, but not in the same way she had when she'd been confronting me in the newsroom. This was more a gesture of self-disgust.

I didn't say anything, hoping that my silence would encourage her to keep going—that was a trick I'd learned from my reporter friends at the newspaper, and it turned out it worked pretty well with girls, too.

"So my dad is a professor here at Allenhurst, in the classics department." Ah, so that explained why her parents had seen the newspaper. I'd been wondering about that. "Jason was one of his grad students. I met him when he came here to do a PhD five years ago. I was seventeen, and he was twenty-two. I was still in high school, living at home in Boston with my parents." She took a long drink of her beer before continuing. "My mom is the quintessential faculty wife. She's always sort of taking care of my dad's students— having them over for dinner, helping them get settled when they arrive, that sort of thing. So this guy Jason arrives, and well…I guess I developed a little crush on him. He was charming, and he seemed interested in me, and much more mature than the guys at my high school." She huffed a laugh tinged with bitterness. "He took me to my high school prom, if you can believe it, because I couldn't get a date on my own."

"I can't believe it, actually."

She shot me a bewildered look.

"I'm sorry, but I don't believe you were incapable of getting a prom date." When she just narrowed her eyes at me, I help up my hands. "What? It's the truth." And it *was*. I would have thought that with her mixture of confidence and beauty, she'd have them lined up around the block.

"So anyway, that's where it started. And that's probably where it would have ended—it was mostly just teenage infatuation on my part—but my parents got…really invested in the idea of us as a couple. Of course, I was too young to get married, though I think my mother would have been perfectly happy if I'd married him right out of high school. But I wanted to go to college, and my dad could hardly object to that, at least not without being a *total* hypocrite."

The way she emphasized *total* made me think her father must have had different standards for his male grad students like Jason than he did for members of the fairer sex. I could see how that would rankle. That was one thing about me: I meant it when I said that I loved girls. Having hung around with so many of them, both ones I was dating and all the newspaper girls—not to mention practically sharing a brain with my twin sister—I'd had an education in the sexist double standard of society. I wasn't out campaigning for the ERA or anything, but I had a pretty good idea of the barriers a smart college girl faced, even in 1984.

"And then I told them I wanted to do an MA, so…here I am," Laraline said, holding her beer bottle up in what seemed like a resigned-shading-into-bitter toast she clearly meant as the conclusion to her story. "Anyway, Jason and I are…taking a break this semester."

I wanted to protest. That might be the end of the story, but there was a whole lot missing from the middle. *My parents got really invested in the idea of us as a couple?* What the hell did that mean? And how can you be "taking a break" from a person and also be planning to marry that person? I mean, I certainly was not the poster boy for committed relationships, but that seemed pretty messed up, even to me. The way she said it suggested that the "break" had not been her idea.

But I got the sense that if I pushed too hard on either of these questions, if I tried to fill in the blanks in her mystifying story, she'd shut down, so I settled for talking around what I actually wanted to know. "Where is Jason now?" I wasn't the type to get worked up over injustices, but part of me wanted to find this dweeb and punch some sense into him. I mean, get married, break up, whatever. But string along girl like Laraline? No. That was not okay.

"He's finishing a postdoctoral fellowship in Greece—which is partly why this MA thing worked out. The timing is good—we both finish at the same time, and then he'll get a professorship somewhere."

I wanted to ask, *And what about you?* But there was something about this girl that had me circling around what I really meant, like probing around a wound but avoiding its actual center. But before I could think of another, more innocuous question, she stood, moved into my tiny kitchen, and set her empty bottle down on the counter. She was clearly getting ready to go, so I met her at the door with her bag.

She rummaged around in it and produced a pen and a

scrap of paper on which she proceeded to scribble something. "You want to call me about the photos?"

"Yeah." I took her number. There was one more question
I really wanted an answer for, and hell, I was just going to
ask it. "Who was the guy in the picture?"

"Oh," she said, waving a hand dismissively. "No one.
Just this guy Brian."

I smiled. Eff me, but I was happy he hadn't been her
forbidden true love, the Romeo to her Juliet.

She shrugged and smiled sadly. "What can I say? It's my
last hurrah. I wanted to let loose a little this semester."

"So maybe that picture actually did you a favor?" I
asked, hating how tentatively the question came out, like I
had something personally invested in the answer. "Maybe
your parents, having seen it, will…" I trailed off. Will what?
Miraculously realize that their daughter should be free to
determine her own future? Tell Jason, and then he'll dump
her definitively?

She shook her head before I could think of a way to
finish my sentence. "I wish, but that's not how it's going to
go down."

"They're not going to hurt you, are they?" I asked,
suddenly alarmed, thinking back to the rally.

She smiled, but only with her mouth. "Not physically,"
she said, and then she slipped out the door.

LARALINE

No, Dad's methods were not physical, I thought as we rode
along I-90 in silence, Boston-bound. My father would never
call himself a genius, but he didn't demur when other people
did. He lived a life of the mind, reserving all his emotions—

the positive ones, anyway—for the opera. He would never sully himself by mucking around in the corporeal world. The closest he got was when he went cycling with our neighbor John Kerry, the lieutenant governor of Massachusetts.

It didn't mean he didn't have his methods of persuasion, though.

"Laraline," my mother said, coming through the back-yard to meet us. Dad wasn't even done getting his briefcase from the car yet by the time she reached me. She didn't touch me, just said my name again on a sigh. "Laraline."

I knew enough not to speak until we were inside. Another thing Dad didn't do was public scenes. No. All must appear in order. Harmonious. Even at the peak of Phoebe's illness, I never saw his composure crack in public. For that matter, I never saw it crack in private, either.

Dinner was on the table. Of course it was. Getting it there was my mom's job, and she took it seriously. The only time she let herself off the hook was if she was helping my dad with a big, time-sensitive project, like typing up his revisions for a journal article on a tight turnaround. Then she would order food from a restaurant, though sometimes that wasn't necessary, as she usually had a few homemade dinners in the freezer for just such "emergencies."

After my father said grace and the chicken scaloppine—my father's favorite, which meant its appearance was no acci-dent—and Caesar salad were served, he turned to me. "Well?"

"I'm sorry," I said, because no matter what else happened, I had to apologize. I was Dove, the peacemaker, so I was always sorry when I was with my family. Even if there wasn't anything specific to be sorry about, there was always Phoebe. Though she'd been dead eight years, I wore the weight of her like a second skin. Which is why it was funny that Tony had commented on my posture that first time we met. I should have been crumpling under that weight. I *felt* like I was crumpling.

"What you seem to fail to understand," said my father, "is that, to quote Donne, no man is an island. No man is free to conduct himself according to his whim."

You are, I wanted to say. *You are an island. You are free.*

Also: *I am not a man.*

"It would be one thing to bring shame solely upon yourself," he went on. "But you have brought shame on all of us. On me. On your mother. On Jason."

I wanted to protest. To say that the courtyard kiss had nothing to do with Jason—with any of them. To say that, in a roundabout way, it had been Jason's idea. But my parents didn't know about the "break" he had suggested. They wouldn't understand.

So I fell back on my refrain. "I'm sorry."

"Sometimes I don't think you understand how hard it is for Jason," my father went on, "being who he is in such an overwhelmingly white field." My father was talking about Jason, of course, but he was also talking about himself. In telling Tony about my situation, I'd glossed over the details, because trying to explain the way my father identified with Jason, viewed him almost as an extension of himself? Well, it would have sounded lame even to my own ears. "To be black in America in 1984 means that to be considered average, you must be above average. To be considered great, you must be outstanding."

I understood all that; I wasn't an idiot. Hell, I was facing the same thing in my own not-super-diverse art history department. But it never occurred to my father to compare our experiences, because to him, my master's degree was a lark I was being indulged in, not the launchpad for a career.

"Jason needs to be beyond reproach," my father said, "and so do those around him."

"Your behavior will reflect on him," my mother said, summing up her entire existence in one short sentence.

"I know," I looked down at my Chucks.

"I console myself that Jason is on a dig in Argilos," my father said, "so it's highly unlikely that news of your…indiscretion will reach him."

There was nothing else for me to say, except to apologize again. It was what I would have done a year ago. But suddenly, I was feeling that two "I'm sorrys" were enough for one evening.

"I've spoken to Professor Malcolm," my father went on, "and he says your work isn't suffering."

My cheeks flamed. The fact that my father occasionally consulted with my MA advisor was an unending source of humiliation. It was like he thought I was a child, and he was attending parent-teacher conferences. The fact that he held no such conferences with his own students' parents didn't seem to register with him.

"Of course it's not suffering," I said. I'd kept my tone neutral, but the way his eyes hardened told me I'd overstepped. But honestly, one meaningless kiss with a boy had no bearing on my academic work.

"Nevertheless," my father said, "I'd like you to stay at home for the next few weeks. I'll drive you in any day you need to be on campus."

"No," I said, suddenly frantic. I couldn't be stuck here. I would suffocate in the house with them for so long. "I… have evening study groups I can't miss."

It was a weak excuse, and he stared at me for a long time before conceding—which he did not with words, but by picking up his fork. "I spoke to Jason last week. He told me he plans to speak to you at Christmas, at the BLO gala. He asked for my blessing."

It shouldn't have been a surprise. Jason had all but told me he would propose over the holidays, and of course the annual gala of the Boston Lyric Opera that he and my father so loved would be the perfect venue. It wouldn't occur to Jason that since I wasn't an opera fan, perhaps the gesture would be better undertaken elsewhere.

I wanted my father to ask me about Brian. That kiss hadn't meant anything, but how did my dad know that? For all he knew, I was in love with the boy. The truth was, he didn't care. My feelings had no bearing on the situation.

All my dad saw was the future he had decided on—the future he and Jason had decided on. A future built by men.

And all we were doing was waiting for it to arrive.

So of course he didn't ask about Brian. Because it was assumed that whatever the story was behind that kiss, it wouldn't be happening again. It was assumed that I would fall in line.

And I would. Because I knew that when I went upstairs, the stairwell would be lined with pictures of Phoebe. Because I knew that my mom cried every night. Still. All these years later. I heard her, which was, frankly, part of the reason I didn't like being at home. It was why I always brought my Walkman when I visited and cranked up the volume and fell asleep with the headphones on. But it was never loud enough to block out what I knew, which was that my mother went to the solarium late at night, after my dad was asleep, and, wrapped in a giant afghan, sat on the sofa and cried for her dead daughter.

It was the only emotion she ever showed that was her own. Otherwise, she was a sponge, absorbing my dad's moods, then arranging the world to best manage them. She was his helpmeet in every way. By day, anyway.

I couldn't face it tonight.

I forced myself to continue eating at a normal pace. When I was finished, I called Cynthia. It was a lot to ask, but I had no other choice. I couldn't spend the night here.

"Thank you for coming to get me."

"No problem," Cynthia said as she pulled away from my parents' house. She was so short that watching her drive was amusing. She was like a tiny Muppet, straining to see over the dashboard. And her '71 Datsun was such a junker that I wasn't convinced she wasn't secretly doing the Fred Flintstone thing, where she was powering the car with her legs.

"Still, it's a three-hour round-trip," I said through a smile. Just being around her made me feel better.

"Which is why I knew it must be important." She glanced at me with a look I knew was an invitation to talk.

I shrugged. "They were upset—no big surprise. I just… couldn't stay there any longer."

She pressed her lips together. Cynthia disliked my parents. It was a reflection of her loyalty. "You know, you can always stay with me. Beyond your graduation, I mean."

"Cynthia…" My voice broke. "I…can't."

She nodded and grabbed my hand for a quick squeeze before returning it to the steering wheel.

Another reason I loved her. She didn't minimize the situation. She knew the stakes were high. Standing up to my parents would almost be like coming out of the closet. They would disown me. She understood that if I didn't fall in line,

I would lose my family—and, just as significantly, they would lose me, their only surviving child.

"So!" she said as we puttered onto the highway, the car protesting the acceleration. "A boy called for you just before I left!"

"Brian?" I dreaded her answer. Why was this so hard? Why couldn't I kiss a boy and have it not be a big deal? I was sure Jason wasn't having these problems on his "break."

"Nope!" Cynthia trilled, and my stomach fluttered. It could only be one person. No other guys had my number.

"Who was it?" I tried to sound casual.

"Tony Bianchi."

"What did he say?" I prompted when she didn't follow up with additional information.

"Who's Tony Bianchi?" she countered.

Tony Bianchi is the epitome of tall, dark, and handsome. Tony Bianchi is Goth Ken in nerd glasses.

"Just a guy who's helping with this campaign to get the board of governors to adopt a new sexual assault policy."

"Um, what?" she said, her tone censorious.

I got it. We told each other everything, and this was a lot of previously unreported info. My only excuse was that it had been a very long two days. "I've kind of decided to take this up as a cause," I said. "You remember two years ago when that football player was accused of all those date rapes?"

She nodded. It had been big news, broken by the campus newspaper.

"And then there were all those protests when they didn't expel him, or even call in the cops initially? And then it got worse when there was that sex scandal that caused that student to kill herself?"

Another nod.

"So the board is apparently studying some new policy alternatives. Danielle's group is launching a big campus PR campaign. Tony's a photographer who's helping us create some of the material."

"Photographer?" she echoed, her tone incredulous. Damn. I had been hoping she wouldn't make that connection, but Cynthia was as smart as they came.

I sighed and slumped against the seat. I wasn't sure why I was being so cagey. It wasn't like anything had *happened* with Tony. "Yep."

"Well, well, well," she said in a tone that suggested she was letting the matter drop, but only temporarily.

"Cynthia," I prodded. "What did he say?"

"He said he knew you were out this evening but asked me to tell you has a contact sheet for you to look at whenever you're ready."

TONY

When I'd vowed to buckle down, concentrate on to my schoolwork, and stay away from girls, I hadn't counted on the fact that I might have no say in the matter. Hadn't factored in the possibility that one of them might just show up at my door at ten-thirty on a Friday night looking like she'd just come from the Last Supper instead of dinner with her folks.

"Laraline?" I stepped back to let her in, taking in her sad eyes. It was like something inside her had been stomped on, some inner light dimmed.

"I'm sorry. I should have called."

"It's no problem." I was glad to see her. Like, stupidly glad.

"I didn't think you'd have the photos done so soon."

I'd gone over to the darkroom at the *Examiner* right after she'd left that afternoon. I hadn't been able to concentrate on studying. "I only have a contact sheet. I thought I'd get your feedback." I was pretty sure those words had never passed my lips before—I wasn't a feedback kind of guy when it came to my photography. "You want to see?"

She nodded.

I was proud of the shots, though *proud* probably wasn't the correct word for pictures of a girl with a black eye. But, as promised, I'd managed to get several arresting images I was pretty sure wouldn't show anything that identified Kari when they were enlarged. I led Laraline to the counter in my kitchen, where the light was brightest, and handed her a magnifying glass. "We need to decide which ones to print. Whichever we end up using, you have to imagine the image with a design treatment around it—your message, some kind of call to action."

"Call to action?" She put the glass to her eye and hunched over the contact sheet that showed all the images from our session in miniature.

"Yeah, like what do you want people to do when they see the image? That's essential. Otherwise it's just an image for its own sake."

"Right." She pointed to one image. "I like this one the best."

It was my choice too, a stark one in which Kari wore a defiant expression. That Laraline agreed with my vision pleased me. "Okay, I'll enlarge that one, and we can make sure we like it. So this is going to be a poster, right?"

She didn't answer, kept staring at the contact sheet, and then she reached out and ran her finger along its edge. "What do you think of a zine?" she said.

"What?"

"A zine." She turned to me. "It's like a homemade, Xeroxed magazine."

I knew what zines were; I'd just been momentarily confused by the abrupt segue. "You want to make a zine?"

"I'm an art history student, right? Both BA and MA, so that's, like, soon to be six years of art history." She turned to me, and her eyes had changed. They were bright with… hope? Happiness? Regardless, this was what she was supposed to look like. I knew it, somehow, even though I didn't really know her. "I can pontificate about art, but I've never actually *done* any."

"So you're thinking a zine that calls attention to this sexual assault policy?" I could see it.

"Yeah. We can do the posters, sure, but think about those pillars on the quad that everyone posts their stuff on. They're covered over multiple times every day. Any individual poster gets lost in the crowd almost the instant it's up. And, honestly, Tony, I'm so sick of…"

"What?" I prompted when she trailed off, because I wasn't sure anymore if she was still talking about the zine.

"I'm so sick of old men making all the decisions." She pressed her lips together, hard, after she spoke, like she was afraid she'd said too much.

I still wasn't sure we were talking about the zine. I remembered that disjointed story she'd told me about her fiancé. About her parents being really invested in the idea of her and her boyfriend getting married.

"Anyway," she said, the urgency gone from her tone. "I was just thinking that if, instead of posters, I did a really compelling zine…"

"It could really make people pay attention," I finished. "Be something they're curious about." She wasn't wrong.

"If it was done right." A slow smile blossomed. "If it had, say, an art director type, a creative person, someone who really knew how to create powerful images."

"Oh no," I said, physically taking a step back. "I'm not doing any extracurriculars this semester."

"So you say."

"Laraline, I'm not like you. I'm not a good student. I'm in year five of my undergrad." I didn't want her to think I was dumb, so I hadn't mentioned that fact before, but I needed her to understand what was at stake for me. "I *have* to graduate at the end of this term."

"Right," she said, and just like that, the light in her eyes went back out. "I forget that for normal people, graduation is something to look forward to."

"What happened with your parents?" I asked, once again substituting a more benign question for the one I really wanted to ask, which was: *Who* are *you? Why are you being so…acquiescent?* The Laraline I knew, the one who had, powered by righteous anger, nearly broken down the door to my darkroom on our first meeting, was defiant. She would never stand by passively and let herself be subsumed by an unwelcome future.

She closed her eyes like people sometimes do against painful sights. "Nothing happened with my parents."

"Bullshit," I said, which caused her eyes to fly open in surprise.

"It doesn't matter," she said.

"It obviously does," I countered, though I wasn't sure why I was getting into this with her.

"Why do you care, Tony?" she said, voicing the very question that I should have been asking myself. "It doesn't concern you."

"It does if we're going to be working together on *Rise*."

Oh, shit. Where had that come from? I had to fight the urge to clamp my hand over my mouth.

"*Rise?*" she asked, cocking her head.

I heaved a big sigh. "The zine we're going to make? Is that a dumb name? I'm sure you can think of something better to call it."

And, as quickly as it had disappeared, the light in her eyes was back, and she threw her arms around me.

I was in deep shit.

CHAPTER SIX

LARALINE

I was going to kiss Tony.

I had decided that the other night, at his apartment, when I'd impulsively hugged him. I didn't do it then, but that was when the idea had taken hold, and it had not let go.

I mean, why not? I'd already decided the Semester of Fun was going to involve some indiscriminate kissing. My first effort had been a bust, but that didn't mean the concept itself was flawed. And I was going to be spending a lot of time with Tony over the next few weeks, it looked like, so it only made sense that I should add him to my list of kissing conquests, for efficiency's sake if nothing else.

"Here," he said, sliding over a mock-up of our zine he'd made out of blank paper. "Do two staples in the middle, I'm thinking?"

We were at Kinko's working on the cover, and then we were going to plan out the content.

His hand touched mine when he passed off the booklet,

and it made me shiver. He must have felt it too—whatever "it" was—because he glanced sharply at me.

Yeah, I was going to kiss Tony, but I'd have been lying to myself if I said it was only because of proximity, because he was handy. Tony had...put the whammy on me or something. In a matter of days, I'd gone from thinking of him as an entitled jerk to noticing stuff like how he gnawed on his upper lip when he was concentrating—and how the upper lip in question was plump and dark pink, almost the color of cherries. Spending a bunch of time with him the last couple days working on the zine had shown me another side of him. Or maybe it wasn't "another side," maybe it *was* Tony, and I'd refused to see it for some reason, because I'd been so angry at him when we first met. Regardless, he'd proven to be intelligent and thoughtful. And, as I'd noticed when he was photographing Kari, there was a quality of carefulness about him. Like he moved through the world with consideration, sensing and adjusting to the emotions of others. Maybe it was all that Goth music. Regardless of its cause, it was strange. I wasn't accustomed to having someone so attuned to me.

"You want to get out of here?" he asked, his voice lower than normal, husky. "Now that we've got the cover mocked up, we can discuss content anywhere, I'm thinking."

My own mouth had gone suddenly dry. It was like all the moisture in my body had moved...elsewhere. I squeezed my legs together against the thrumming of my pulse there.

Then I nodded.

He started tidying up the communal work surface, putting tape, staplers, and glue back where they belonged. "It's almost five, and I could do with some dinner. We could hit the Allenhurst Tap Room." He spoke casually, but then he looked up and caught my gaze, his hazel eyes glittering. "Or we could grab a pizza and head to my place."

"Let's go to your place. More room to spread everything out if we want to look at the zine." I wasn't sure why I added that last sentence. I had already decided on my course of action, and it wasn't like I needed an excuse.

As we made the twenty-minute walk across campus to a pizza place near his apartment, we talked about the zine. We had decided to keep the first issue tight, in the name of getting it out soon. We would run the picture of Kari on the front, an interview with a sexual assault survivor, and a short piece on the board of governors vote along with their contact info and suggested text for a letter. I was going to write the content, and Tony was going to design it.

By the time we got to his apartment with our large pepperoni-and-mushroom in tow, we had pretty much discussed everything we needed to, and each had our marching orders.

So there was really no reason for me to be here.

He unlocked his door and held it for me. The apartment had been put back to rights. The last time I'd been here, he'd moved everything around to make room for the photo shoot. What struck me this time was how the main room was dominated by a big bed. He had a tiny kitchen in which he had two chairs but no table, and there was a small book-case with a TV on top of it in the main room, but that was pretty much it. So the apartment was, visually anyway, mostly bed. Most students I knew had twin beds, but not Tony. He had a queen-size one with a big, fluffy, yellow-green duvet that looked like the color of spring. It seemed…incongruent.

But, I reminded myself, I didn't really know him. Maybe

he was exactly the kind of person you'd expect to have a fluffy chartreuse bed.

He led me to the kitchen and offered me a beer, which I accepted.

"To *Rise*," he said, turning around and leaning back against the counter. We clinked our bottles together.

TONY

Yes, I was in deep shit, and it was getting deeper by the minute.

Not only because here I was, entertaining Laraline in my apartment after I'd sworn up and down to Tanya and everyone—to *myself*—that I was eschewing girls this year, but because I was nervous.

I, Tony Bianchi, was *nervous*. Not to be too much of a conceited dick or anything, but I didn't do nervous. It simply wasn't in my repertoire. But here I was, having to wipe my sweaty hands on my jeans so I didn't drop my beer.

I also had no idea how to get us out of the kitchen. Probably we should eat, but my stomach was unsettled. There was also the question of *where* we would eat. I usually ate on my bed in front of the TV, or, if I was eating something messy, I set up a TV tray in front of one of my two chairs—but I only had one tray.

And generally if I had visitors… Well, the bed sufficed. Which wasn't to say that I didn't like to wine and dine my guests, just that it was usually in the context of…other activities. So, yeah, the bed tended to do the trick.

But Laraline. I wanted her, and I couldn't have her.

That was a new one for me.

Usually if a girl struck my fancy and turned out to be off-limits, I moved on. Plenty of fish in the sea and all that.

I *certainly* didn't agree to make a zine with her, invite her over for beer and pizza, and then have a panic attack about whether she would think I was coming on to her if I suggested that the bed was the only place in the apartment to eat dinner.

"You see them in Boston in '80?" Laraline's question jarred me out of fretting. I followed her gaze to my Cure T-shirt.

"I did."

"That was a great show."

I lifted my eyebrows. "We were at the same show four years ago?" The idea was strangely compelling. Like the universe had been trying to throw us together. It was hard to believe I hadn't seen her, though. "Were you there alone?" I was probing about this Jason guy, I would freely admit—to myself anyway. I wanted to know more about the man who was going to get Laraline.

"I was," she said. "Most of my friends are more into Wham! and, like, Cyndi Lauper."

"Jason not a fan either?" As soon as the question was out, I regretted it. Why did I care what kind of music Jason liked? I didn't, of course, but Jason was like a loose tooth that I couldn't stop probing with my tongue.

"No. He's more into opera. He and my father—that's their thing. Anyway, Jason and I haven't really…dated very much."

"You haven't dated the guy you're engaged to?" I swear, her life was like some kind of cheesy, melodramatic soap opera.

She sighed. "I was too young, really, when he first arrived on campus. He took me to prom, as I told you. And then he was only physically here for the first year and a half of his degree, when he did his coursework. The rest of the time he was in Europe doing research. He'd come for visits, of course, and we'd...hang out."

"So how do you get from that to *engaged*?"

"It's hard to explain."

"Try me." I didn't know why I kept pushing. Also, there was still that congealing pizza. I could at least offer her a chair if I was going to interrogate her—give her the TV tray and stand at the counter with my own slice. But I didn't. I just stared at her, willing her to answer.

She took a long pull from her beer before speaking. "Well, to begin with, my dad is kind of obsessed with Jason. Like, he's the son he never had or something. Or maybe it's more that he sees Jason as an extension of him—like a protégé. Regardless, he and my mom were thrilled with Jason's interest in me."

"You're an only child?"

She shook her head before letting it fall forward like it was too heavy to hold upright anymore. She was silent so long I was just about to ask her if everything was okay. Then she finally said, "I had a sister who died."

The anguish in her tone was a lance to my chest. "Oh, Laraline, I'm sorry." I wanted to touch her so badly that my hands got jumpy.

"Phoebe, her name was," she continued, as if she hadn't heard me. "She was seventeen when she died, and I was fifteen, though she'd been sick for three years before that."

The math wasn't hard to do. Her sister dies, and a couple years later, this Jason guy swoops in. Her parents love him. He's the prodigal son they didn't know they were missing, and if they can pair him up with their surviving daughter, he really *will* be their son. As screwed up as the situation was, it was starting to make a warped kind of sense.

Laraline still wasn't looking at me. I wanted to see her face, to reach out and tilt her chin up, but I knew I didn't have the right to touch her, to take what she didn't want to give.

"She had leukemia. I was going to donate bone marrow. It looked like I was going to be a match, but then, at the last minute…it turned out not to be true." She lifted watery eyes to mine, giving me the eye contact I'd wanted so desperately a moment ago. It just about undid me, to see that much anguish on that beautiful a face. "I don't think my parents ever forgave me."

I grabbed her hand. I couldn't hold myself back anymore. "You can't think it's your fault."

"I don't. Not really. I just…"

I saw it all then, too clearly. "You're trying to make up for it." She was going to marry this Jason guy not just because her parents wanted her to, but because she had some twisted idea that it was her destiny.

She smiled sadly. "I know it sounds dumb."

"It doesn't sound dumb." Well, it *did* sound dumb. But families are complicated. And I had no idea what I'd do if my sister died. I'd probably become a little irrational, too. I was still holding Laraline's hand, which felt like an overstep, so I let go of it, which was harder than I would have liked.

But then, just as her hand was about to slip away, she grabbed *my* hand, halting my retreat. She set her beer, which had been in her other hand, on the counter next to me. Then, quite methodically, she took mine out of my other hand and did the same.

Then she kissed me.

Holy God, Laraline was kissing me.

My reaction was all out of whack. She was kissing me softly, gently, her lips moving against mine almost chastely, but everything inside me roared to life. I was hard in an instant, and a herd of rhinos seemed to be having a party in my stomach. I gave it a few beats to make sure this wasn't some kind of "thanks for helping with the zine, buddy," kiss that she'd miscalibrated, but when she didn't seem to be retreating, I settled my hands on her cheeks and deepened the kiss slightly, hoping she'd come along with me.

She did. She opened her mouth, and I couldn't stifle a groan as our tongues touched. It had been so long, and she felt so good. The way she sighed into my mouth did some kind of caveman thing to me. I was stupidly proud that I had the power to summon those noises from Laraline, who, at least in my experience with her, was usually so poised and self-contained.

She took a step closer. I'd purposefully been touching her only with my hands. I didn't want her to feel my raging boner and think I was a jerk. But there was nowhere to go. My butt was against the counter, and she had me cornered.

But she didn't seem to mind. "Tony," she breathed, breaking our kiss as she pressed her body against mine and buried her head in my neck. I gave in and wrapped my arms around her, holding her tight, letting the feel of soft breasts against my chest permeate my being. God, she felt so *good*. I needed a better word. She felt…like everything.

But then it was over. Too soon. What could I do when she pulled away, though, but let her?

I expected a big speech, something about how that had been a mistake. Maybe she would invoke Jason.

But instead she just flashed me a smile—a full, unreserved grin that almost took my breath away. Then she turned and took a piece of pizza from the box, walked the few steps to the main room, flopped down on my bed, and said, "*Dynasty* is on. Can we watch it?"

"Sure." I laughed. I'm not really sure why. It could have been because the whole thing was so surreal. Making out with Laraline and then watching TV—*Dynasty*, no less, my sister's favorite—like nothing had happened.

Or it could have just been because I was happy.

Goddamn it.

CHAPTER SEVEN

LARALINE

"What's got you all Up With People this morning?" Cynthia asked as I ran around the apartment tidying up. And humming.

Shoot, I was humming.

"Nothing."

That was a lie. What had me twirling around like a Disney princess was that kiss.

Like, wow, that kiss.

It wasn't like it was my first kiss. Jason and I had had sex, for God's sake, so we'd kissed a bunch of times. And I'd had a boyfriend when I was fourteen, before Jason came on the scene.

And of course there had been the courtyard kiss with Brian.

But somehow, none of them had come even close to Tony. I mean, my body had responded to kisses before—they had been pleasant—but there was something about Tony that made me...want. So much. But at the same time,

I didn't feel any pressure with Tony. The stakes didn't feel high, which was a relief.

Probably I should have been panicking. This was a huge complication—in terms of the zine and in terms of my whole life. I should have been worrying about how to backpedal, how to apologize.

But I wasn't doing any of that.

In fact, I was planning on doing it again.

"Can you move this to your room?" I asked. Cynthia had a drying rack of damp laundry set up in the living room.

Her eyes narrowed. "Why?"

"I'm expecting someone."

"And would this someone have anything to do with you flitting around here like you swallowed a rainbow?"

A knock on the door saved me from having to respond. My stomach flipped as I ran to answer it.

Most of the boys at Allenhurst dressed like they'd stepped off the set of *Miami Vice*, but not Tony. He was wearing his usual uniform of jeans and a black T-shirt, but this pair of jeans wasn't ripped, and this T-shirt wasn't faded. It had the effect of making him seem dressed up, like he'd tried harder than usual.

"You are not going to believe this," he said, pushing past me and waving a piece of paper. "I just saw this pasted to a telephone pole on my way over."

I tried to wipe the grin off my face, I really did. Cynthia was looking at me with her eyebrows raised, and I didn't need her on my case. But it was impossible not to smile at Tony when he was all enthusiastic about something. You didn't even have to know what it was to be infected by it.

He was also so...delicious. That tall lankiness. That floppy hair that he kept pushing out of this face. Those long fingers. My cheeks heated as I thought of them resting on my face two nights ago. Realizing they were both looking at me expectantly, I tried to tamp down my lust long enough to perform introductions. "Tony, this is my roommate, Cynthia."

He turned a grin on Cynthia and said, "Great to meet you. You can help me convince her."

"Convince me of what?" I said.

He handed me the piece of paper he'd been carrying. It was a call for candidates for student positions on the college's board of governors.

My first, instinctual reaction was *yes*. My whole body leaned toward that paper. This was the natural next step in my campaign to take on the sexual assault policy. It almost felt like fate that Tony had found out about this opportunity on his way to see me. Everything was falling into place.

"Oh my gosh, yes!" exclaimed Cynthia, who'd been reading over my shoulder.

"You guys aren't saying I should run?" I asked, just to make sure the abrupt arrival of this unprecedented ambition in my heart wasn't foolish.

"That's exactly what I'm saying," Tony said. "The zine is great, but if the goal is to influence the board of governors, to have a hand in the decision-making, what better way than to—"

"Become one of them!" Cynthia finished.

"Yes. I can help you with campaign posters. We'll take an amazing picture of you. We can use the zine, too, to advance your candidacy."

"This is so bitchin'!" Cynthia exclaimed. "Can you imagine? Dove for student governor."

Dove.

With that single word, reality came crashing down

around me. It was a reminder of why I couldn't run, of what I couldn't have. Cynthia must have seen something in my face, because she quickly corrected herself. "Laraline, I mean! Laraline for student governor!"

But it was too late.

"I can't," I said, fighting the urge to hang my head. I didn't want to look at them, to see them judge me when they realized what a coward I was. I wished Tony had never seen that poster.

"Why not?" Tony asked. "It's perfect. They have one undergrad seat and one grad."

"But I'm graduating in the spring," I said weakly, trying to come up with an excuse that was actually legitimate.

"It's a one-year term," said Tony, who apparently had an answer for everything.

"But..." I trailed off, barely able to form words through the lump thickening in my throat. I hadn't known about this opportunity five minutes ago, so how was it possible that I now wanted it so much? How was it possible that the idea of having it taken away from me felt like losing my toehold in the world?

"But your father will lose his mind." Cynthia finished my sentence. Strangely, though, her voice didn't hold any of its characteristic sympathy. Cynthia was usually so kind, so compassionate. Cynthia usually understood.

When I thought of Jason, of having to go wherever his career took us after we were married, the thing that really gutted me was the idea of giving up my best friend, the one person in all the world I could rely on absolutely. When we'd finished our undergrad degrees and I'd gone on to do an MA, Cynthia had stuck around instead of doing the logical thing and moving the seventy-five miles up the highway to Boston. She was going to wait, she always said, until I was done. "Then I'm gonna move to wherever Jason gets a job," she would joke. "I'll be like your spinster cousin you have to take in. They need engineers in Greece, right?" I always laughed, but inside, gratitude and affection welled up so much that I feared that one of these days my laughter was going to turn into tears.

Maybe today was going to be the day, because tears were certainly threatening.

"I, uh, have to get going," said Cynthia. "I have a work thing."

What? She was making that up. It was Saturday morning, and I knew she didn't have a work thing. She'd been talking earlier about making a new batch of cookies today. Which meant she was just straight-up abandoning me. I whipped my gaze to her face, but she wasn't looking at me. In fact, it seemed like she was making a point of *not* looking at me as she scooped up her purse and moved toward the door. I guess I hadn't been imagining the edge I'd heard in her voice earlier.

I shot her a look but she was already halfway out the door, waving over her shoulder. "Nice to meet you, Tony." She still didn't look at me, but she added, "I think you should do it, Laraline."

"Wait a sec." I moved to the door just in time for her to shut it in my face.

My Cinderella-at-the-ball mood from a few minutes ago had disappeared completely, like the gown and carriage after midnight. I was left with a chasm of disappointment topped off with the knowledge that I'd just been abandoned by my best friend.

I burst into tears.

You know, just to make my wretchedness complete.

I was still facing the door, so I had my back to Tony. I

used both hands to swipe the tears away, but they were coming too fast.

"Laraline," he said softly, coming toward me.

I didn't want him to see me like this, so I hunched my shoulders, trying to curl inward on myself, but he kept coming. When his hand made contact with my shoulder, I started crying harder.

"Don't cry." He put his hands on my shoulders and turning me. I gave up trying to resist and lifted my face and straightened my spine.

"Oh, sweetheart," he said, opening his arms.

I walked into them.

It was just a simple hug. But, at the same time, there was nothing simple about it. It was profoundly comforting. His arms were so strong, and the way he stood there, unmoving, made it feel like he would hug me forever if I wanted him to.

It was also unsettling, though, because the more time passed, the more something inside me started to change. It was like something was moving through his body into mine, something bracing and warm and alive. Something that felt a little bit like…courage?

"I'm going to do it." I spoke quietly, but loud enough that it was out there. Loud enough that he heard.

He pulled away just enough to meet my gaze. A grin unfurled across his face, and I felt it reflected on my own.

Then I laughed. Partly because: holy shit, I was going to do it! But probably also because of the tsunami of changing emotions that had washed over me in the last few minutes, emotions beyond words. I felt like the only response to that absurd pendulum of feeling was laughter.

He laughed too. What *was* it about this guy? It was like

we were mirroring each other, like we didn't need words to be tuned into what was happening.

Which was why, when our lips met, it was impossible to say who was kissing whom. We were kissing each other.

And unlike last time, it wasn't soft and gentle. It was exuberant and needy and insistent, and as he licked deep into my mouth, want shot through me. *Want.* It was turning out to be the theme of the afternoon. It was heady, wanting. Wanting things and *taking* them instead of sublimating your desire.

Tony was stroking my back as we kissed. I reached around and grabbed one of his hands, guiding it under the hem of the loose sweatshirt I was wearing. My bra clasped at the front, so I undid it before withdrawing my hand. He paused for a moment, his hand under my shirt but not moving, and I feared I had made myself ridiculous. But just as humiliation was about to crowd out lust, he slid his hand up to my breast and hissed. He actually hissed, like I was hurting him.

It made me laugh. He chuckled too, but it stopped being funny when he kneaded my breast, letting his thumb flick back and forth over my aching nipple as he ground out, "God, Laraline, God."

And then we were staggering toward the couch, a tangle of grabbing hands, each frantic to touch the other every-where. Somehow, before we landed, we managed, working together, to get my shirt off.

He pushed me gently onto the sofa and sank to his knees on the floor in front of me. Without giving me chance to catch up to what was happening, he fastened his mouth to one of my breasts.

"Oh my God!" I exclaimed. Jason had touched my breasts, of course, but he had never put his mouth on them.

So I hadn't known—hadn't known that the warm wetness of a tongue could have such an effect. Moisture gathered between my legs, where a deep-seated ache was growing almost painful.

Or maybe it was just *Tony's* tongue in particular, because he seemed to know exactly how much to tease with light flicking before he opened his mouth wide and sucked.

It was all I could do not to shove my own hand into my shorts.

But then I thought, why the hell not? Wasn't I in this situation to begin with because I had, uncharacteristically, decided to take what I wanted?

So I did it.

Tony growled in what sounded like appreciation, though he pulled back. "Let me," he said, after a moment, sliding his hand over mine. "Show me."

I was burning with embarrassment, but it was okay because I was also burning with lust, with the intoxication of taking what I wanted, and that second burning was stronger than the first. So I switched the position of our hands, putting my fingers on top of his, and showed him how I liked my clit stroked.

He was a fast learner. Within a minute or so, I was shaking and shuddering. He left his hand on me, left it there beneath my shorts and watched my face intently as the aftershocks rippled through me.

Now that the interlude was over, the embarrassment that had been waiting in the wings took center stage. What was supposed to happen now? He had a hard-on. I wasn't sure... what I was supposed to do about that. "I'm sorry," I whispered.

"You're *sorry?*" he echoed, his incredulous tone at odds with his smile. "Why?"

I wasn't sure. Maybe that although I wasn't opposed to returning the favor, I was scared shitless. Maybe that it had happened at all? No, that wasn't right.

Actually, maybe I *wasn't* sorry. Maybe I was just so used to apologizing that it had become my default emotion, elbowing its way into my brain even when it hadn't been invited to the party.

"Well, I'm not." He hoisted himself up to sit beside me on the sofa. He leaned over, refastened my bra, and handed me my sweatshirt. All the while, he just kept smiling. "Okay, we have work to do," he said.

"We do?"

"Yeah. We have to talk about issue two of *Rise*." He winked. "And we have a campaign to plan, too. Did you know I'm a political science major?"

"Um, no," I said, willing my brain to dislodge itself from my still-tingling body and pay attention to what he was saying. "I guess I assumed you were a studio art major, what with the photography."

"Nope. Poli sci major, art minor. There's this crazy senior portfolio thing they make the art majors do that I was keen to avoid." He winked, still smiling like a kid at Christmas. "So let's get to work.

"Do you want to…wash your hands first?"

"No." His smile disappeared, replaced by something else more dangerous. "No, I do not."

CHAPTER EIGHT

TONY

I spent the week walking around with a perpetual hard-on. There was no cure. Well, there was a cure, but that wasn't happening.

But it was okay. It shouldn't have been, though, and that was the odd thing. Blue balls...weren't really my thing. The world was big, and it was full of amazing girls, I'd always thought, so why waste time with one who wasn't interested?

But that was before Laraline. Before I'd seen her transform herself into a confident woman powered by righteousness. Before I'd seen her cry. What it sounded like when Laraline cried... Well, it was something I never wanted to hear again.

So, in the past week, we had settled into a rhythm. Almost every hour I wasn't in class, we spent together. We would work on the zine or on her campaign, putting up posters or handing out leaflets outside big classes. Then we would go to my apartment, and I would make her come. Usually more than once.

I was addicted to it.

It made no sense.

She kept protesting and was forever trying to grab my dick, but I never let her. I would always take care of her and then retreat. Even though it was, objectively, ridiculous, I had my own warped logic. I wanted her to feel good. Hence the multiple orgasms. I also wanted her to stick around. I was afraid that if things got too heavy, she would bolt. She'd told me that *Laraline* was Latin for "seagull," and I did think of her like a bird. If I moved too swiftly or suddenly, she would fly away, back to her father. Back to her fiancé.

So I'd gotten all weirdly selfless, sexually speaking.

There was no precedent for that. But if I started to worry too much about what it might mean, I shoved those rogue thoughts out of my mind. Gave Laraline another orgasm.

"In conclusion," she said, her eyes darting around as she stood in front of my bed. We were practicing a speech she'd be giving at a student assembly tomorrow. She smiled sheepishly. She couldn't remember her line. There were note cards, but they were in the kitchen, and I was on the bed, playing her audience.

She was adorable as she scrunched her nose and searched for the missing line. After a few beats, she made a silly face and shouted, "In conclusion, fuck the patriarchy!" Then she clapped a hand over her mouth.

I laughed and applauded.

"I'm usually not like this," she said.

"Like what?" I asked. *Beautiful? Breathtaking?*

"Bold," she said.

"But you are," I protested. "Remember the first time we met? You nearly broke down the door to my darkroom."

She flopped down on the bed beside me. "I know it

seems that way to you, but I'm really not. Or at least I haven't been historically. You don't know the real me."

I raised an eyebrow. Her comment would have stung if I had believed it. I thought it was possible, likely even, that she had it backward, that I *did* know the real her, and that *Jason* was the one who didn't. I did know what she was talking about—I had seen a hint of a more timid version of Laraline that day she'd cried in her apartment. But anyone who knew her at all, in any genuine way, knew that wasn't *her*.

But I would never say any of that for fear she would fly away. So I settled for teasing—the type of teasing that would work to my advantage. "Let's see." I worked her shirt off and rolled on top of her. "Is this the real you?" I kissed her breasts, but only briefly, because I was aiming for the waistband of her leggings. Sitting up on my heels, I worked them over her hips, grabbing her underwear as I went. "Or maybe *this* is the real you," I teased as I headed back up, using my hands to open her legs and kissing her right on the clit. She shrieked and tried to squirm away from me, so I relented and backed off.

There she was, Laraline, naked in my bed. She was gorgeous. Her long legs, her flat stomach, her small, perky breasts with their generous brown areolas. I wanted to touch all of her, all at once.

This was why I was doing everything I was doing. Eschewing orgasms in favor of beating off in the shower after she left my place. Breaking my rules about avoiding girls and non-class-related activities. I'd failed my last American Lit test, for God's sake.

But I didn't care.

"Can I take your picture?" I asked.

"What? Like this?" She scrambled to a sitting position.

"I'll develop it myself. No one will ever see it," I said, though I knew she would probably not agree.

"Why take a picture if no one will ever see it?"

It was a good question. It reminded me of Jenny's adage that a picture should tell a story or it should be... "A work of art. Because it would be a work of art. Because *you're* a work of art. Because I want to..." I wanted to remember, later, when she was gone. I didn't say that part, though, because the mere thought of it nearly tore me in half.

But she must have known what I meant, because she nodded. "Okay."

Surprised by her acquiescence, I hopped off the bed to grab my camera, but then I thought better of it. "Actually, I think I'd rather shoot you after you come." Yes. She'd be all sated and mussed. I would look at that picture for the rest of my life and know that I'd done that.

"We have to stop doing this."

"What? No." Frantically, I started mentally backpedaling. I didn't need a picture, not if it was going to mean the end of our time together.

She laughed, scrambled off the bed, and went over to her bag. I was working up a speech to convince her to stay when she produced a box of condoms from her backpack. "I'm not really sure why you refuse to let me touch you, but honestly, Tony, you're giving me a complex. I don't want to do this anymore unless we both enjoy ourselves. Do you just straight-up not want me? I know I don't have a ton of experience, but...I can't be that bad at it."

There wasn't even a moment of indecision. Not a single one. Somehow I had conditioned myself, this past week, to resist sinking into her and taking my pleasure, but that was before she was standing in my apartment naked *holding a box of condoms* and starting to get the very, very mistaken impression that I didn't *want* her.

So I smiled and said, "Okay."

"Okay?" Her eyes widened, and I grinned. She had been expecting an argument.

So there we were, staring at each other, me fully clothed and her fully naked.

I felt like a goddamned kid in a candy store. I might end up with a belly full of regrets later, but I could no longer be made to care.

"Yeah," I said, clearing my throat because my voice was catching a little. "And for the record, I don't think I've ever wanted anyone more than I want you."

She walked toward me, one corner of her mouth quirked up in a self-satisfied smile, a gentle but determined hunter. I shivered even though I was the one with clothes on. I'd thought she might kiss me, given the intensity with which she was looking at my mouth, but when she reached me, she went straight for the hem of my T-shirt and pulled. I raised my arms to help her, my nerves on fire with anticipation, but also trepidation. It wasn't that I doubted my ability to satisfy her—I'd done that thoroughly and often in recent days. It was more that I felt like this might be a turning point. She was wading farther in, coming out to where I was waiting in the dangerous rapids. Once I started holding onto her out here, how did I know I wouldn't drown once I had to let go?

She tossed the shirt behind her, and it landed on the bed. Then she ran her fingers lightly down my chest, stopping at my stomach, which I was holding tense to try to anchor it. To anchor us, out here in the rapids.

"Your stomach is trembling."

I followed her gaze. I had a not-bad body, and my abs were fairly defined. But she was right. I was shaking.

"Are you scared?" she asked.

I nodded. It was the truth.

She didn't ask any more, didn't press me to elaborate, and I was glad. She simply reached for the waistband of my jeans, making quick work of the buttons on my fly. My boxers-clad erection sprang free, and she laughed, like she was a kid delighted by a gift.

I took over, pushing jeans and boxers together down and stepping out of them. Usually I had no problem getting naked, being naked. But I have to admit that I paused for a few heartbeats as I was bent over, postponing standing back up and subjecting all of my self to her inspection. As absurd as it was, I felt like she could see through my skin, see everything, and, more to the point, that she would find me lacking.

My worries were assuaged at least somewhat by the fact that as I finally stood, she gasped. Just like with my stomach, seeing myself through her eyes was excruciating. My dick was okay in terms of size, I thought, and of course I'd learned over the years the power of fingers and tongue. But my family, in the way of the old country, didn't practice circumcision, and I'd discovered that most of the girls at our WASPy school hadn't had a lot of experience with uncut dicks. Not that any of them ever said anything negative to me, but I could tell that a couple had been a little taken aback initially.

It didn't seem to matter to Laraline. She kept looking at me with that half-smile, her pupils dilating before my eyes. Nevertheless, I stroked myself a few times, retracting the foreskin; then I held a hand out to her. She put one of hers into my outstretched palm, like we'd just agreed to dance.

Pulling her into my arms, I whispered into her ear, "Never. I've never wanted someone this much."

"You say that to all the girls," she breathed, even as she tilted her head back. She liked having her neck kissed, I'd learned. Before I settled in to worship it for a while, I shook my head in a rather exaggerated "no," making sure to rub my whiskers over her tender skin, making sure she *felt* my denial.

The abrasion made her moan softly, and as I kissed it better, I placed a hand between her legs, stroking her folds. "Mmmm," I hummed against her neck. "You're so wet already."

She hissed a breath in, making a noise I had come to unambiguously identify as evidence of her arousal, but then she swatted my hand away.

"Let me touch you," she said, and before I could react, she was. Oh God, she was. Laraline was touching my dick, squeezing it lightly, experimentally, but it was nearly enough to make me double over in pleasure-pain. I wasn't going to last long, and I sure as hell wasn't going to waste this opportunity by coming in her hand as we stood in the middle of my room. So I grabbed her hand and led her to the bed, pausing to grab a condom on the way. Then I sat back against the headboard and, keeping hold of her hand, guided her so she was straddling my lap.

As she rubbed her slick pussy over the tops of my thighs, I buried my face in her breasts.

"Tony!" she cried as I took a nipple between my lips, grazing it slightly with the edges of my teeth, loving the way it instantly hardened in my mouth. I bit down lightly, then immediately switched to licking it, covering as much of her areola as I could with my tongue.

When I switched to the other breast, intending to repeat

my pattern of assault followed by soothing, she cried out and escaped my mouth by straightening her upper legs, so she was still kneeling but no longer touching me. I felt the loss of her wet warmth like someone had torn off a strip of my skin, and instinctively bucked up after her, even as a growl I hadn't been able to swallow signaled my displeasure.

"Shhh," she said, leaning up and over to reach the condom—I had placed it within arm's reach, but it had migrated away a bit because of our wrangling.

The movement brought her left hip to within inches of my mouth, so I grabbed her ass to anchor her, hunched over, and fastened my mouth over the bony point of her hip.

"Unnhhh," she moaned. "Tooonnny." I loved when she said my name like that, stretching it out like it tasted good —like it tasted as good as she did to me. "Put this on," she said, pressing her palm, with the condom underneath it, flat against my chest. I was going to demur, to set it aside so we could prolong the foreplay. I mean, in some ways, there was nothing I wanted more than to do as she asked, to sink into her and let myself be carried away on a wave of pleasure. But even though I was going to give in this time, I still wanted to make things good for her—no, I wanted to make things *great* for her.

But then she pulled away entirely, leaving my body cool everywhere it had been touching hers, and said, "Please."

I couldn't resist that. So I did what she'd asked, and had myself sheathed in a matter of seconds. Then I held my hands up, intending to take a breath, to assess, to figure out exactly what was going to come next.

She took my hands, reminding me, once again, of dancing, but then she laced our fingers together and sank down on my cock. I didn't know if she'd ever done this before. She hadn't gotten specific about what kind of experience she'd had with Jason. So I kept still, wanting to give her a chance to adjust if she needed to. It took all I had, because being with Laraline was so much better than I'd imagined—and I'd dialed my expectations up pretty high. But she was so tight, so hot, and when she was fully seated, a rush of tears gathered in the corners of my eyes.

She seemed not to need the reprieve, because she moaned as she ground her pelvis against mine. Then she retreated, kneeling back up, leveraging herself against my hands. At the top, just when I was about to slip out of her, she reversed direction, impaling herself on me again, and my resultant gasp pushed some of those waiting tears out of my eyes. I reached out and pressed a thumb against her clit, mimicking her approach-and-retreat movements, rubbing harder on the downstroke and letting up a bit each time she pulled away.

The rhythm we'd established was slow and punishing and…perfect. I kept my eyes on hers. At the top of each stroke, she was taller than I was, and at the bottom we were eye to eye. In tracking her movement, I gave a long, slow nod.

A *yes*.

"Yes," I said, because there didn't seem to be any option other than to verbalize the word that had taken over my whole consciousness. All there was was the pressure of pleasure, gathering in my lower back, my balls, gathering everywhere, including my heart.

All there was…was the yes.

CHAPTER NINE

LARALINE

My father came to the speeches the next day.

Of course he did.

Had I really thought I could run for board of governors without him finding out?

It was like with that issue of the paper. You couldn't hide anything from him on campus.

I didn't see him, though, until I was already on the dais, sitting on a row of folding chairs facing the small audience of students that had assembled to hear the candidates speak. There were only two of us vying for the grad student spot. The undergrads had gone first, and the last one was speaking. As the first of the two grad student candidates scheduled, I was up next.

So I had a few minutes to watch my father watching me. Of course, he didn't express any outward displeasure. That wasn't his style. But the way he stared at me unwaveringly, with his lips pressed together, signaled everything it needed to. Last time I'd displeased him, he'd accused me of bringing shame upon him and Jason. That time, of course, had been over a kiss. This was a campaign speech. I couldn't say exactly how he would twist a campaign speech into something contemptible, but he would. By the time I was done, I'd be left feeling cheap. Like I'd disappointed him. Again. And maybe this time beyond repair.

I had a wild thought of simply getting up and leaving. I mean, why not? At that moment, it seemed like me dropping out of the race was the inevitable outcome, so why not save us all the heartache and get it over with?

But then a movement in the front row caught my eye. Tony had spent the duration of the previous speeches lounging against the back wall. Every time I glanced over at him, he'd already been looking at me, and he would nod and flash me a smile. It was an encouraging smile, on the surface of things, but it also contained something secret, something just for me. It contained heat. It *created* heat, a mirroring warmth low in my belly, as my thoughts slipped back to where they were pretty much constantly these days —his bed.

But now he was elbowing his way into the only empty seat in the front row, and the mild commotion was enough to attract my attention, to break the connection between my father and me. Tony folded his long arms and legs up so he could fit in the small folding chair and raised a new face to meet my gaze. The smile was gone, and so was the heat. Or at least the sexual heat was gone. It had been replaced, or maybe only temporarily subsumed, by another kind of urgency. He looked at me expectantly from beneath his glasses, like he was waiting to hear what I had to say. Like what I had to say was important.

And as the student emcee stood to introduce me, Tony nodded at the appropriate spots in my bio, but he kept looking at me, almost like he was daring me to break eye contact with him.

I knew what he was doing. He was giving me something to focus on besides my father. I don't even know how he knew what was happening—he wouldn't have known my father by sight, but I suppose what I'd told Tony about my situation combined with the appearance of a fifty-something black man in a suit was enough of a tell. Tony was smart. He kept talking about what a bad student he was, how he kept failing his classes, but he was smart in a different way. He saw things other people didn't, had the ability to look inside a person, to the real kernel of them, to identify the part of them that was trying not to drown.

Well. What did a person do when confronted with a lifeline?

She took it.

Light applause broke out, which was my cue. I rose on shaky legs and walked to the podium.

Keeping my eyes on Tony, I said, "Good afternoon. My name is Laraline Reynolds, and I'm running for the Allenhurst College board of governors."

TONY

My aim had been only to get Laraline through her speech.

Something had happened to her when her father—for who else could the older guy who'd caused such a change in her demeanor be?—arrived. I couldn't really explain it, but he seemed like he had some kind of power over her. Which was fine—the guy could flip out about his daughter running for student office if he liked, but he wasn't going to do it in such a way that he ruined the speech she'd worked so hard on. He wasn't going to humiliate her in public.

Not on my watch.

So I'd pushed my way to the sole empty chair in the front row and fixated on her like some kind of besotted stalker, willing her to stay focused. The speech was the important thing, at least for now. And it worked. She spoke strongly and calmly, and since she was offering a specific platform including but not limited to the sexual assault policy, she came off as thoughtful and well-versed in the issues.

Let's just get through the speech, I'd thought, *and leave the rest of it for later.* Let the students see her talk, hear what she had to say, and *then* she could have it out with her father if need be.

Except now I was revising that stance.

After she sat down, she started looking at her father again. Well, she alternated between looking at him and looking at her feet. I kept trying to catch her eye as her opponent, the last slated speaker, laid out his qualifications. But she never looked my way. I'd lost her.

By the time the emcee formally closed the event, her father had made his way to the base of the dais and was waiting to intercept her.

She was wearing high heels. If it had been me, I would have offered a hand to help her down the four steps from the stage. Her father did nothing, just stood there with his arms crossed and his eyebrows lifted. The moment her feet hit the ground, he took her elbow and guided her to one side of the room. I kept willing her to look over at me, so she'd know I was waiting for her, but she didn't.

There were lots of students milling around talking among themselves and to the candidates. A few glanced in her direction, which probably meant she was missing an opportunity to work the crowd. That concerned me.

But not as much as the way she was…deflating. Her father was talking at her. Not yelling. Talking. But *at* her, not with her, and she was getting smaller.

I couldn't let that stand.

So I made my way over there and busted right in. It was probably rude.

"Laraline, there are a couple students waiting to speak to you."

She jumped a little. I was sorry to have startled her but glad that my intrusion had rendered her father speechless, at least momentarily.

I seized on the break and stuck out my hand. "Tony Bianchi, Laraline's campaign manager." I made up that title on the spot, but I wanted him to understand that she had people on her team. "Nice to meet you, sir. You must be so proud."

"I'm not sure *proud* is exactly the word." His eyes narrowed as they moved between his daughter and me.

I put my hand on Laraline's back and pressed gently, hoping it would be enough to propel her out of her father's orbit. I wasn't naïve enough to think that removing her from his presence would solve everything, but at least I could talk to her before she had to face him again.

To my surprise, it worked. "Right," Laraline said, as if woken from a trance. "I have some people I have to speak to." She shot me a small smile that probably wasn't a good idea, because her father did not miss it. "We can talk later, Dad."

I kept my hand on her back as we walked away.

CHAPTER TEN

LARALINE

I loved having sex with Tony.

I was as surprised as anyone. Well, not surprised that it felt good. I mean, I'd started with the idea of merely kissing him, of adding him to the list I had imagined expanding on all fall: "Boys Laraline Kissed During Her Semester of Fun." But I'd quickly realized that what Tony had to offer was a lot more powerful than a mere kiss.

God, just thinking about him got me wet.

So, yeah, by the time election day rolled around, two weeks after he'd come to my apartment with that flyer, we were embroiled in a full-on sexual affair that was blowing my mind.

The surprising part was that I wasn't freaking out. I had somehow managed to compartmentalize things so that I could carry on with Tony without feeling guilty about it. Quite the opposite, in fact. I almost felt like I had a responsibility to grab as much of him as I could for as long as I could. Because in the neighboring compartment, on the other side of the partition I'd erected around our relation-ship, there was a part of me that recognized that this was as good as my life was ever going to get.

So I was just...open. I let myself sink into experiences with Tony. I walked around naked in his apartment with no shame. I directed him on how to please me, and I asked for direction in return.

The more astonishing thing was that whatever alchemy he'd unleashed that had made me into this confident, free person was spilling out *beyond* the bedroom, outside the confines of Tony and me. It was the only way I could explain why I had walked away from my father's disap-proving tirade after the speeches the last week. Why I had returned neither his nor my mother's calls in the days since.

Why I had won the election.

Why I, Laraline Reynolds, was a member of the board of governors of Allenhurst College.

I didn't have official confirmation yet, but the moment Tony walked in the door, I knew.

I was at the Allenhurst Tap Room. Cynthia and I and a few of our other friends had headed over after classes to settle in and wait for Tony, who'd promised to use his news-paper connections to get the latest edition hot off the press, the one that would contain the results of the election, and hand-deliver it.

And, oh my God, when he burst through the door, carrying a stack of newspapers, he didn't even have to say anything. It was all over his face. I saw him before he saw me, and watching him search the crowded bar for me was incredible. The big, goofy grin he wore told me I'd won, but it was more than that. It was the intensity with which he scanned the throng before he found me. It reminded me of that time I'd watched him from afar at the Take Back the

Night rally, when he'd been prowling around, his graceful, lanky body propelling his fierce intellect through the space, looking for something he'd know when he saw it.

Except this time, the thing he was looking for was me.

I didn't think I'd ever been the object of such determined focus before. It made me shiver. It made me want.

When his eyes finally landed on me, he pressed his lips together, hard, kind of like you do when you're trying not to laugh, and lifted his eyebrows. He dropped the newspapers he'd been carrying on the bar next to him and opened his arms as if to say, *Voilà!*

I ran to him. What else could I do?

His arms came around me so hard it almost hurt, and he physically picked me up so that my feet were dangling a few inches off the floor. "You did it," he whispered in my ear, his voice not joyous or celebratory, but low, knowing. Raspy.

I corrected him. "*We* did it." I could feel him start to protest, but I shut him down. "I couldn't have done this without you," I said, tapping his arm to get him to release me.

"Nah, I just took some pictures, put up some posters."

"No," I said, struggling to articulate the way he had made me...fearless.

He must have understood even without me saying the words, because he said, "Thanks," and then, after holding my gaze for a long moment, "What are we drinking?"

I shrugged. "I was having a beer, but..."

"But what?"

"But I also have beer at my apartment."

It only took a second for him to get what I was saying. We never hung out at my place—he'd only been there that one time, the day he showed up with the flyer about the elections. By unspoken agreement, we always ended up at his apartment. He probably thought it was because his place was private, and I had a roommate. But really it was because it was easier for me to suspend my disbelief if we confined our affair to his apartment, which was mostly bed anyway. It was easier for me to live parallel lives if each one didn't overlap too much.

"Let's go." He grabbed my hand and spun around, heading for the door he'd just come in.

We didn't even make it half a block before he stopped and kissed me.

That was another thing I didn't really do—engage in public displays of affection. The courtyard photo had taught me a lesson. I knew the likelihood of running into my dad was low, but still, the prospect haunted me.

But for once, I didn't feel like imposing my rigid rules. I just wanted to be a girl. A happy girl celebrating a victory. A girl kissing a boy.

So I let him push me up against a tree and devour my mouth. Not just there, but several times along the way. Each time, he'd grab my hand and tow me along for a block or so, but then it would be like something would bubble up between us and he couldn't wait any longer. *We* couldn't wait any longer.

Each time, I would light up inside, like a string of fireworks was being ignited inside my belly.

"Didn't you want a beer?" I mumbled laughingly against his lips as we kissed our way in the door to my building.

"There has been a reordering of things I want," he rasped, pushing me back against the wall of mailboxes in the lobby.

"I don't have any condoms upstairs," I said, tilting my head back so he would do that neck-nuzzling thing that made me so crazy.

"Then I'll just eat you out all night long. What do they say? To the victor go the spoils?"

I laughed, partly because his persistence was so endearing and partly because I couldn't believe this was my life, and threw my arms around him.

He picked me up again, but because we had more room than we'd had in the crowded bar, he actually twirled me around in a circle, which only made me laugh more.

"I—"

"Laraline."

Whatever it was Tony had been going to say was interrupted by someone else saying my name. Tony clamped his mouth shut and set me back on my feet.

"Mom?" I whirled, but of course it was her. I'd know her tentative, resigned voice anywhere. My mom had never been to my place. She rarely came to campus, and when she did it was to attend events with my father. I wasn't even sure she could drive anymore. I mean, she had her license, but as far as I knew, she hadn't driven since Phoebe died, since those days we were all back and forth to the hospital so frequently, it felt like we lived in the car. It was like her world had shrunk so much she was functionally agoraphobic.

So I was stunned by her independent appearance. Part of me, the fatalistic part, had expected to run into my dad for some kind of reckoning. But not her.

"You haven't returned my calls."

I closed my eyes for a second, like maybe if I didn't see her, this unlikely person standing in the lobby of my apartment building, I could somehow will her away, could keep my two worlds from colliding, one from tainting the other.

"I won, Mom," I said, opening my eyes to take in her worried face. I assumed she knew about the election, because otherwise why would she be here? "I won a seat on the college's board of governors."

She smiled, and for a second I thought maybe it was going to be a happy smile. A proud one, even. But it turned wistful before it ever had a chance.

"You must be Mrs. Reynolds." Tony took a step toward us, which put him a foot or so behind me. I could feel him there, just like that night at the pay phone. But unlike that night, I *knew* him now. I knew what he could do for me. I wanted to lean back against him, to take comfort in his solid mass, to gather some of the courage that only he seemed to be able to give me, but I didn't dare.

"Do you know where your father is, Laraline?" My mother ignored Tony. This was alarming, because if there was one thing my mother always clung to, no matter what else was going on, it was manners. She'd written a prompt thank-you note for every casserole that had been delivered in the days following my sister's death, for heaven's sake.

"Where?" I asked, though I was certain I did not want to know the answer.

"He is meeting with Larry." Larry was our family's lawyer. That couldn't be good. "Larry, and the CEO of the Boston Lyric Opera, and the BLO's lawyers," she added.

"Okay." In addition to being a big BLO fan, my dad was a donor, so he was probably shoveling some money at them. That wasn't unusual.

"You know they're undertaking a big capital campaign? For the new building?"

I didn't, though I probably should have. We attended the opera's Christmas gala every December, and it always included speeches and fund-raising appeals. This year, to hear my father tell it, it was also supposedly going to involve Jason proposing to me. As such, I'd been avoiding thinking about the opera generally, so I wasn't surprised I didn't remember the ins and outs of its fund-raising goals.

"Your father is giving them a million dollars, Laraline."

Wow. I was shocked. I knew we did well—my dad had literally written the book on the art and architecture of classical antiquity. The undergrad textbook was in every classics program in the country, probably in the world. And my mom's family was well-off, so I assumed she'd inherited money when her parents died, but…still.

Regardless, I wasn't sure why we were having this conversation now. There was a shoe waiting to drop, was there not?

"In return," my mother said, her voice quavering, "the new performance space will be called the Phoebe Reynolds Theater."

Oh, my poor father. It was a lovely gesture, but if he'd known his late daughter at all—the real her, not the ghost he had built up in his mind—he would have been giving that money to the Sox to create the Phoebe Reynolds Bullpen or something.

"Okay, Mom," I said, "that's great. But maybe we can talk about it later, because—"

"He's doing it because he says it's important to have at least one daughter who isn't a disgrace."

Only then did she look at Tony, and not for very long, either. Her eyes just slid over to him, lingered a moment, and came back to me.

Me and my shattered heart.

Tony moved closer to me, tried to touch me, like he knew how much I needed his solid mass holding me up.

I had been deluding myself. What had I thought was going to happen anyway, after Tony and I went upstairs?

Yeah, we'd have some spectacular sex, but what about tomorrow? And the next day, and the next?

I waved Tony off before he could touch me. The damage was done, and he couldn't help me now.

My mother had gotten what she came for.

CHAPTER ELEVEN

TONY

It had been two months, two weeks, and six days since Laraline left school.

It still wasn't any easier.

"It's not any easier because you're in love with her."

"What?" I bolted to a seated position from where I'd been lying on my bed. My accuser was my sister, Tanya, who'd come to visit for Thanksgiving. I hadn't made the trip back to New Jersey for the long weekend, in theory because I was concentrating on my studies. That was a lie, though, because I'd never been doing this well academically. Amazingly, I was on track to get A's and B's in all my classes.

The truth was that getting out of bed, on the bus to Boston, then on a train, was too much effort. Dealing with my huge extended family was too much effort. After Laraline left, *everything* was too much effort. So I did nothing other than plod through the days and study at night.

"Look at you. It's like you're a husk of a man. Ha!" Tanya threw her head back and laughed. "I always thought that phrase sounded melodramatic, but, look! It's actually a thing!"

I smiled in spite of myself. If there was anyone in the world who could make me feel less broken, it was my twin. All that twin shit you hear about—secret languages and ESP? It was all true for Tanya and me. Which was probably why, after spending the actual Thursday of Thanksgiving with our parents and extended family, she'd impulsively taken the train up and arrived at my door. She had known something was wrong, just not exactly what. So she'd "borrowed" our parents' VCR and we'd rented a pile of movies and holed up eating Chinese food in my apartment all weekend.

"I am not in love with her," I said. "She just…kind of… threw me for a loop."

"Uh-huh."

"I'm trying to watch the movie," I elbowed her and pretended I was really into a training montage of Mr. Miyagi imparting his wisdom to Daniel-san.

"No you're not. You've been lying there having a monologue about this girl for the past ten minutes." She tilted her head and affected a teasing, nasally voice. "'Laraline gave this amazing speech—you should have seen it.' 'Laraline did this interview for our zine.' What's next? 'Laraline walks on water'?"

I rolled my eyes.

"Remember when I was on campus, and you were always on my case about boys, always trying to scare them off if they were interested in me?"

"That's because you have terrible taste in boys." And because I knew boys. I was one, after all.

"No." She dismissed me with a wave of her hand. "It's

because you had an enormous, sexist double standard: You never wanted a boy to treat me the way you treated girls."

I blinked, caught off guard by her aggression. My sister and I bickered all the time, but we were never truly cruel to one another. "I never treated anyone poorly!" I protested, thinking of my fridge full of Tab, and hell, my pretty wicked oral skills.

"I'm not saying you were an abuser or anything, Tony. There's nothing wrong with casual relationships—which is what I was always trying to tell you." She slugged me again. "Goose, gander, and all that. But that's not the point. The point is, you always told me to hold out for a guy who loved me. And do you remember that one time we were arguing after you'd run off some guy I was talking to at one of those Delta Chi parties, and I asked you how I was supposed to know if a guy loved me if we'd only just met? Do you remember what you said?"

I did not. I didn't even remember the conversation, though it sounded like something I would have said. I did have a double standard when it came to my sister, and I wasn't sorry about it.

"You said, 'If he's the kind of guy who could love you, he'll want to be with you all the time. You'll always be in his mind. He'll get interested in rowing. He'll get up at the ass crack of dawn to walk you to practice.'"

"Uh, okay." I did sort of remember that conversation now. My sister had been on the varsity crew team when she was a student here, and rowing had consumed a lot of her life. "So what's your point?"

"My point is: look at you! You've turned into this feminist crusader!" She laughed and gestured to my kitchen table.

"Oh, shit," I whispered as my stomach dropped. My

table was covered with issue number four of *Rise*, which I had printed but had yet to distribute. I'd kept putting out the zine. I'd talked Danielle, who had, in Laraline's absence, helped me with content.

"What else did I say, again?" I asked. "Give me that little speech one more time."

"She'll always be in your mind."

I nodded, because I didn't trust my voice. Things had gotten kind of iffy in my throat.

"You'll want to be with her all the time."

Shit.

That's why I was so miserable. That's why I was, uncharacteristically, acing my classes.

I was in love with Laraline.

I guess I hadn't recognized it for what it was because I honestly had no experience with the emotion. Sure, I loved my family, and my sister was like my other half, but this... this was different. It was a full-body longing. No, that wasn't right. It was a full-heart longing. A full-*being* longing. Everything in me was magnetic, and Laraline was my north pole. My true north.

"Don't cry, Ant Man," Tanya said, wrapping her arms around me.

The old nickname made my heart wrench. Ant Man was what Tanya called me when we were kids. Ant was a short form of Anthony, my full name, and the "Man" had been added sometime along the way. She hadn't used the endearment for years, and for some reason, it made me think of Laraline and her dead sister. I couldn't imagine life without Tanya. What had the last two months, two weeks, and six days been like for Laraline, alone with her parents? At least, I assumed that was where she was. She'd written me a letter, thanking me for all my help with the zine and the campaign, and telling me she was finishing her master's thesis from off campus and forfeiting her spot on the board of governors. There had been no return address on the envelope. I'd tried to talk to her roommate, but she claimed to know nothing. The wagons had been circled.

"I'm not crying," I said as I surreptitiously used my sleeve to wipe my eyes before pulling out of Tanya's embrace. I flopped back on the bed. "Leave it to me to fall in love with the one girl I can't have." There was no point in pretending anymore, at least not with my sister.

"Who says you can't have her?"

"She's getting engaged in nine days."

"*What?*"

See, the fact that I knew that it had been two months, two weeks, and six days since Laraline left was just the inverse of the fact that I knew that it was nine days until the Boston Lyric Opera gala, at which Jason was supposedly going to formally propose.

I filled Tanya in as best I could about Jason—and Phoebe. By the time I was done with my sad, twisted tale, we were both lying on our backs on my bed, staring at the ceiling while the *Karate Kid* credits rolled and Survivor sang about the moment of truth.

Tanya turned to look at me. "Well," she said, "I guess that means you have nine days to figure out what the hell you're going to do about this."

I didn't need nine days. I didn't need nine seconds. I, Tony Bianchi, was in love with Laraline Reynolds, and now that I realized that, now that I had my head out of my ass, I wasn't giving up without a fight.

I hopped off the bed and picked up my phone. My fingers were clumsy as I stuck them in the holes to turn the dial. But that was okay. I had to clear my throat so I'd be able to talk around the lump in it, but that was okay, too.

"Hello?"

My heart sped up. "It's Tony."

There was a long pause, long enough that I worried that she'd hung up. But then, a sigh. "I've told you, she's not taking my calls. I even tried to go to her parents' house, but no one answered the door. I don't know where she is, Tony."

"Cynthia," I said, "I do. I know. Or I know where she *will* be. In nine days."

Another pause. Then another sigh, but this one wasn't shaky; it was determined. "All right. Then let's go get our girl."

CHAPTER TWELVE

LARALINE

It had been two months, three weeks, and one day since I left Allenhurst.

It still wasn't any easier.

"Sweetie?" said my mom, looking at me quizzically in the mirror in the ladies' room at the Boston Lyric Opera gala. She was standing behind me futzing with my hair—she hadn't liked the way one side of it was sitting against my head. I sighed and angled my neck so she could reach it better. I thought my hair looked best natural but had easily given in when she'd asked me to have it straightened for the gala.

"Did you hear me, sweetie?"

"I'm sorry." I shook my head. "I must have been daydreaming."

"I asked if you were nervous."

"No."

I wasn't nervous, because I was dead inside.

In a way, I was looking forward to the evening, because

at least it meant forward motion. I'd been living in limbo since I'd left school. No, since I'd left *Tony*. Because if there was one thing I had vowed as my chains were locking into place, it was that I would always be honest with myself. The lie that I had to live would not extend into my mind, which would remain my own. So, in a warped sort of way, I was ready to get on with things.

Though life wouldn't truly move on until the fall, when Jason would take up a faculty position at Rutgers. Until then, I still had to finish my thesis, though that was well under way. My father had insisted that I move home and finish writing there. When I needed to meet my advisor, he drove me to campus and waited in the car like I was a child at a junior high dance. It should have angered me, but I was resigned. Numb. The dove was back in her cage, and it was easier to just forget that there had ever been a life outside it, a life of sunshine and rallies, of open sky and…love.

When my mom had come to get me that day, I'd had a horrible glimpse of the future. If it had been my dad, arriving with his silent rage, things might have gone differently. I might have let myself fall back against Tony, confident that he would catch me. But my mother. Standing there in her plaid skirt and cardigan, clutching her car keys to her chest like she'd just trekked the Sahara instead of driven a late-model Volvo to a leafy college campus. To know my mother was to know the courage that journey had taken. I'd thought then, as I did all the time now, of her crying in the solarium at night, rattling around the house, waiting on my father as her world got smaller and smaller. What my mother had been doing when she'd come to collect me was protecting herself. Grabbing desperately at a future where she had one daughter left, instead of none. Because we both knew that if I refused Jason, if I refused the plan for my life that the men in it had made, I would be as dead to my father as Phoebe was. Worse, even. He was naming a theater after *her*.

So, in the end, I had made my peace with almost all of it. The only thing I still struggled with was the missed opportunity with the board of governors. My own heartbreak was one thing, but letting everyone down, letting the *cause* down—that stung. I didn't know how to make peace with that.

"Rutgers isn't so far," my mother said. There had been no segue, but she hadn't needed one. We both knew what was coming.

"That's right," I said, testing the waters. "You could visit. You could take the train."

"We'll see," she said. She wouldn't come. I'd be alone in New Brunswick, New Jersey, a faculty wife to a brilliant, trailblazing man. I'd be living my mother's life.

"Well, let's get this show on the road," I said, looking in the mirror at the dead-eyed girl with the flat hair. "I'm sure they're here by now." Jason had flown in earlier in the day. My father had left the house in the afternoon to pick him up at the airport, and they were going to meet Mom and me at the gala.

Mom smiled. A real smile that reminded me why I was doing this. Now, in this moment, my mother was happy.

"You look lovely," she said.

I didn't, though. I didn't look like myself. But I formed my lips into a shape that would look, from the outside, like a smile, and said, "Thanks."

TONY

I saw her right away. I had been worried about how to find her. I imagined a huge, cavernous space crowded with people, but when we entered the building, we found ourselves in an anteroom adjacent to the main space. It was a long, narrow lobby of sorts dotted along its length with sets of double doors that must have led to the gala itself—I could hear the buzz of conversation and the clinking of dishes on the other side.

And there she was, on the far side of the lobby. She was so beautiful she took my breath away. She was wearing a green shimmery dress. It was, on the face of things, not very revealing. Though it was short, it had long sleeves and it wasn't low-cut. But it fit her like a second skin, revealing curves that all her slouchy dresses and Siouxsie T-shirts never did. Her hair was different—longer. She looked like a more formal, grown-up version of herself.

I stood straighter and smoothed my tux. It was a cheap rental. I'd been worried about fitting in, and indeed, I would look like a pauper next to her. I would look like a pauper next to *Jason*. God, he was handsome, and as he gestured animatedly, his tux moved with him, like he was as at home in it as I was in my ratty jeans.

And then he fell to one knee at her feet.

Or he started to anyway. Laraline grabbed his hands and intercepted him. Didn't let him make it all the way down to the floor.

Cynthia gasped. "We're too late."

"No," I said, lifting my camera. "We're right on time."
Click.

LARALINE

I couldn't do it.

I was as surprised as anyone. I mean, why had I retreated this far, back to Boston, back to my parents' care, back to my old life—back to my *cage*—if I was just going to upend everything anyway? Why had I given up my seat on the board of governors, if, in the end, I was going to refuse my destiny?

I didn't know the answer. But I did know, as Jason reached into his pocket and started to bend his knees like he was going to sit down—but there were no chairs in the lobby—that I had to stop him. His knee could not hit the ground.

So I reached out to stop him, and then...

I shouldn't have been able to hear that clicking sound over the pounding of blood in my ears. Or over Jason's voice, which was clear and assured as he talked, undaunted by the interruption of his kneeling gesture. He spoke of making him the happiest man in the world, of always remembering the beautiful ceremony we'd just witnessed inside in which my father's gift to the opera in honor of my sister was announced. Or over the opening notes of *Popoli di Tessaglia*, the after-dinner performance, which had just begun inside.

But there it was just the same, a soft but sure sound, tapping at the edge of my consciousness. Something to fall back against. Something that could hold me up.

Click.

I turned. How could I not?

He smiled and lowered his camera. "Laraline. We have to stop meeting like this."

I opened my mouth to say something but closed it when I realized I had no earthly idea what that something should be.

He handed his camera to…Cynthia?

"Oh my God." Seeing my best friend and Tony there together—my two favorite people in the world—did something to me. They were like the visual equivalent of the last meal before an execution. I wanted to run to them. I wanted to grab greedy handfuls of them. I wanted to hold on and never let go.

"The thing is, I want to be the guy in the picture with you, Laraline," Tony said, walking toward me with his palms showing, like I was a wild horse he was afraid would spook and not a tame bird who had been about to lock the door on her own cage.

He didn't know that I'd already begun my flight—my flight back to him.

"I want it to be *me*," he said as he took one more step, which left him standing directly in front of me—and Jason, who said something I didn't hear. "Because you're the greatest person I've ever met." Tony continued. His voice caught, and he cleared his throat. "Because I love you."

I must not have been breathing, the inhale that came then was a huge, gasping, shuddery one, like I'd been trapped underwater and had only just that moment broken the surface.

"I brought you a couple things," Tony said, using his elbow to physically block Jason, who was trying to get between me and him, but otherwise ignoring my presumed fiancé. He produced, to my utter astonishment, an issue of *Rise*. "Number five," he said.

"You kept publishing it," I breathed.

"Of course I did." He handed me a newspaper. "And there's this."

It was a copy of the *Boston Globe*. It was open to the classifieds, and one ad was circled. I struggled to focus on it through watery eyes. It was an advertisement for a junior copywriter at the Boston chapter of the National Organization for Women. "Oh!" I exclaimed.

"Or if that's not right, maybe you can get a job in a museum. Or get a PhD."

I lifted my eyes to his, confused. Was he making a declaration of the heart here, or was he trying to get me a job?

As if he'd heard my silent doubts, he said, "I want you to be mine. I want to be yours. But most of all, I want you to be happy."

"Let's move to Boston," said Cynthia softly. "All of us. I can still be your spinster cousin. I'll live in the attic!" She shot me a lopsided smile. "Or you and I can still room together and you can make Tony prove himself for a while."

"What?" I said, starting to laugh because my mind just couldn't keep taking in all this…possibility.

"We can figure out the details later. You're always saying how the guys at work don't deserve my cookies, aren't you?"

"I passed all my classes," Tony said, grinning.

I smiled back. "Congratulations."

"It turns out not having you around was pretty good for productivity." He held out his hand, palm up. "What do you say?" He glanced at where Jason had been standing, but Jason was now gone.

Could I really do this? Could it be this easy?

"Laraline!"

My father.

My parents and Jason burst through the set of doors nearest us.

"What the hell is going on here?"

"Mom, Dad, Jason," I said, hating how soft my voice was, and how shaky. "This is Tony. I…love him."

"Laraline!" my father said sharply. "Have you no sense of decorum?"

"And you know Cynthia," I said, still wishing my voice sounded more authoritative, but plowing on nonetheless. "I'm thinking of moving to Boston." I glanced at Tony, whose hand was still extended. "And getting a job." Yes, the idea of a job felt right. "I shouldn't have forfeited my place on the board of governors at the college. There's good work to be done, and I should be doing it."

My father exploded. What had I expected? He knew exactly which buttons to push, spitting out the usual accusations about how I was shaming the family, but also new ones about how I was, in my selfishness, ruining this day that was meant to honor my dead, perfect sister.

I should have been immune by now, but his words were as sharp as ever, and they still had the power to wound, to rob me of breath and free will. I tried to keep my head above water. I wanted that job. Or another one like it.

I wanted Tony, the one who always helped me swim against the rapids.

And he was doing it again, judging by the way I could feel someone's gaze on me. I lifted my eyes to search out my anchor.

Then something extraordinary happened.

The gaze I'd been feeling wasn't Tony's, or wasn't only Tony's. It was my mother's. She had tears in her eyes, but she was…smiling? Even as my father continued speaking angrily, she smiled. It was just a little smile, hardly noticeable, but it looked so strange on her face that it functioned like a life preserver, stopping me from tipping overboard and drowning in the churning sea of my father's words, which were still being spewed all around me.

She held my gaze for a moment, then her eyes went elsewhere. I followed. She was looking at Tony's hand. Then she found my gaze again.

Then she nodded, and I saw what was happening. If Tony was my anchor, way out there in the uncharted sea, my mother was giving me the means to swim out to him.

She was giving me up.

Or maybe she wasn't, because she said, "If you're in Boston, I won't have to take the train."

"What?" My father, who still hadn't stopped talking, because he hadn't realized we had all stopped listening, turned to her. It was not usual for her to speak over him, so she'd startled him.

"Nothing," she said.

But it wasn't nothing. It was everything.

I put my hand in Tony's.

He squeezed—tight.

"I don't think Phoebe would want me to live my life in deference to her death." I recognized the truth of the words as soon as I spoke them. In fact… "I think she would want me to live a life big enough for both of us."

"Yes," my mother whispered, and that one nearly inaudible syllable was all the ratification I needed, considering its source.

"Laraline," my father said sharply, "come back inside."

"I can't." I saw now that my father would never see things my way. He was stuck, treading the same rut over and over, holding the rest of us hostage. I could stay stuck with him, safe in my gilded cage, or I could…change.

"Listen to me, young lady," he started, gearing up again, but Jason put a hand on his shoulder and interrupted.

"It's okay, Dr. Reynolds. Why don't you and I head back in? We're missing the performance."

"I'm sorry," I said to Jason. I truly was. We just

weren't...right. Maybe he could sense that—maybe that's why he'd asked for the break this past fall. Still, he didn't deserve this humiliation.

"I'm sorry, too," he said, smiling sadly at me as he took my mom's arm and started leading her back into the ballroom.

After a beat of silence, my father followed.

After the door shut behind them, Tony pulled me into his arms and kissed me, hard and fierce and possessively.

I let myself surrender to his mouth for a long moment, but then I pulled away as I realized Cynthia was retreating.

"Hang on!" I called after her. "Come back."

"It's okay," she said, "I'll talk to you guys tomorrow."

"No!" I protested. "Get over here."

She obeyed, and I pulled her into our embrace, and we had a big, goofy group hug. Happy tears were shed all around.

"Okay," she said after a moment. "I'm really going now."

"One more thing before you do?"

"Anything," she said.

I reached for the strap around Tony's neck, lifted the camera over his head, and handed it to Cynthia. "I need you to take a picture of us."

Then I turned to Tony, and just before my lips hit his, I said, "You are the guy in the picture."

Click.

ACKNOWLEDGMENTS

My editor Gwen Hayes really helped me untangle this book, and in the process sparked a little revelation/existential crisis (I mean that in the best way) about my writing in general.

Polly Watson continues to rule the world when it comes to copy editing. (Though despite her extraordinary efforts, I still don't understand when I'm supposed put a comma after "because.")

Audra North and Sandy Owens provided excellent early feedback and steadfast friendship.

Courtney Miller-Callihan, who remains the best agent in all of agentdom, was relentlessly supportive.

Courtney and Del Dryden straightened me out on darkroom mechanics and the cameras of yore.

Each of the books in the New Wave Newsroom universe is inspired by a song from the 1980s. This one, of course, came from "When Doves Cry." Prince died while I was writing this book, and, as a girl from Minnesota, and a citizen of the world, I still feel the loss. "Life is just a party, and parties weren't meant to last." RIP, Prince.

CONNECT WITH ME

Sign up for my newsletter at jennyholiday.com/newsletter. I send newsletters when I have a new release or a sale, and I sometimes include stories and access to freebies only for subscribers. Or you can find me on Twitter at @jennyholi or visit my website at jennyholiday.com.

Reviews really help authors, not only because they help us find new readers but because more reviews means more favorable treatment by retailers' algorithms. If you're moved to leave an honest review of this book or any of my others on the retailer's site where you bought it, I'd be most grateful.

ABOUT THE AUTHOR

Jenny Holiday started writing at age nine when her awesome fourth grade teacher gave her a notebook and told her to start writing some stories. That first batch featured mass murderers on the loose, alien invasions, and hauntings. (Looking back, she's amazed no one sent her to a kid-shrink.) She's been writing ever since. After a detour to get a PhD in geography, she worked as a professional writer for many years. Later, her tastes having evolved from alien invasions to happily-ever-afters, she tried her hand at romance. Today she is a USA Today bestselling author of all sorts of romance novels: contemporary and historical, straight and gay. She lives in London, Ontario.

www.jennyholiday.com
jenny@jennyholiday.com
Twitter: @jennyholi
Instagram: @holymolyjennyholi
Newsletter: jennyholiday.com/newsletter

BOOKS BY JENNY HOLIDAY

NEW WAVE NEWSROOM

The Fixer

The Gossip

The Pacifist

THE FAMOUS SERIES

Famous

Infamous

BRIDESMAIDS BEHAVING BADLY

One and Only

It Takes Two

Merrily Ever After

Three Little Words

THE 49TH FLOOR

Saving the CEO

Sleeping With Her Enemy

The Engagement Game

His Heart's Revenge

REGENCY REFORMERS

The Miss Mirren Mission

The Likelihood of Lucy

Viscountess of Vice

AN EXCERPT FROM FAMOUS

FAMOUS #1

Seven years ago

Sometimes a wedding was not just a wedding.

This one, in which Evan Winslow's friend Tyrone pledged his eternal devotion to his girlfriend Vicky, was, in fact, a test. It looked like a normal wedding, with white funereal-looking flowers and ill-fitting tuxedos, but it was *also* Evan's Hail Mary pass: one last attempt to hold on to his life in Miami, to his nascent career, to his entire freaking life.

His final experiment to measure how extensive—how *permanent*—the damage inflicted by his father on the Winslow family's reputation was going to be.

Evan had laid low for the past two weeks, hoping the whole "out of sight/out of mind" adage would prove true, and now it was final exam time.

This test had one question: Could Evan attend his friend Tyrone's wedding and not be recognized, not upstage the proceedings with his mere presence?

The answer was no. Fail. Flunk.

Which meant this was it. Today was the end of life as he knew it, which sounded melodramatic but was no less true for it. Because if Evan knew one thing with certainty, down to the dusty corners of his soul, it was that he could not live with the fame—the *infamy*—his father's crimes had brought down on his head. He had already been coming around to accepting the idea that his painting career was done before it had even really started—thanks to the crimes of Evan Winslow Sr., Evan Winslow Jr. was destined to be persona non grata in the art world—but now he'd brought the goddamned paparazzi to his best friend's wedding.

He'd tried to hedge against that prospect, and he initially thought he'd succeeded. He'd spent the night at his brother's place. Evan's brother wasn't in the art world—the family business—having opted instead for life as an overgrown trust-fund baby. So he wasn't getting as much media attention as Evan. Evan had called a cab to his brother's house, timing things so as to arrive at the church just before the ceremony started.

But he'd miscalculated, emerging from the taxi as a limo pulled up and disgorged the bride and her attendants.

He'd held out a shred of hope that the flashbulbs that started going off were actually for the bride. But how many brides hired half a dozen photographers with zoom lenses to photograph their nuptials?

How many wedding photographers yelled things like "Were you in on it too?" and "Will you attend the sentencing hearing?"

So he'd hustled inside ahead of the bridal party and tried to make himself inconspicuous.

Which, of course, had set off a series of whispers among the guests. People talking behind wedding programs, some openly pointing at him. The bride's mother glaring, no doubt because he had upstaged her daughter before she'd even made an appearance.

It didn't even matter that everyone recognized him, really. The fact that he had failed his test was regrettable but not elementally important. Because even if the infamy died down, could he live with the lie? With the notion that everything he had—his luxe condo; his painting ability, honed over years of lessons from the world's greatest artists; his expensive grad school—was all built on lies and paid for with stolen money?

The answer to that question was also no.

So it was time to go. To start over somewhere else. Pack his shit up, transfer to another college to finish his degree—say goodbye to his entire life.

He had no earthly idea how to do that, but that was a problem to be solved tomorrow, on day one of his new life. Right now, the last day in his old life, he had a wedding to attend.

Thankfully, the music changed at that moment, signaling the start of the ceremony. Everyone turned, and he breathed a sigh of relief. For a few moments anyway, there were people in the room who would attract more attention than he would.

He almost laughed as the first bridesmaid appeared. The dress was ridiculous. She looked like a short, puffy, pink mummy. Evan didn't know fabrics, but he suspected that the multi-layered, shiny dress she was wearing had not been constructed from any fiber or dye that occurred naturally in this world.

And there was another one, and another. They kept coming, parading down the aisle in ascending order of height, like caricatures of bridesmaids rather than actual bridesmaids, with their identical upswept hairdos and identical pink heels.

His wrist twitched. They would make a great painting, all of them lined up like nesting dolls.

No, correction: as the final bridesmaid appeared at the top of the aisle, Evan had to revise his previous thought. They would make a great painting, but *she* would make a spectacular painting. He would title it *Bridesmaid Number Seven*.

Tall and thin with long limbs, she was the sort of person people might describe as gangly. It was like someone had taken a regular, average woman and stretched her out like taffy. But she was too graceful to be rightfully called gangly. She had an ease about her, which was rather remarkable, given the packaging and spackling she'd been subjected to.

Evan noticed those sorts of details when a painting was emerging. It was like his brain clicked into some other mode as it swept over a scene, processing, neutrally assessing everything with equal attention, waiting for the jolting spike of feeling that signified the correct take on a subject.

He was a beat behind everyone else standing for the bride because he was still looking at the last bridesmaid. She and her colleagues arrayed themselves at the front of the church and turned to watch the bride process. Her face had interesting angles: sharp cheekbones and slightly unruly brows arching high over eyes that should have been too close-set to be called pretty.

Where would he put her? In a forest, maybe? In her ridiculous pink dress in a forest, Titania styled by Barbie? No. That wasn't quite right.

As the bride passed his pew, he forced his gaze from her tallest attendant and considered his friend Tyrone's soon-to-be-wife with more attention than he had ever found it necessary to bestow on her before. Vicky had the same facial structure as the bridesmaid, but less of it. The cheekbones were there, just not as prominent. The two women had to be related. Sisters, maybe?

As Vicky's father kissed her and sat down, the bridesmaids turned their backs to the congregation, presenting the assembly with a row of identical bows on their backsides, each one a little higher than the one next to it thanks to the arrangement of attendants from shortest to tallest.

He was still thinking about her face, though.

He would start with Yellow Ochre and add tiny amounts of Cadmium Red Light to start with, and then he'd layer in the planes of those gorgeous cheekbones.

It was with a jolt, a great wrenching, invisible blow, that he realized: *no*.

Not that those were the wrong colors, but that he wasn't going to paint her.

He wasn't going to paint anything.

After today, he didn't paint anymore.

* * *

"Is that cute guy in the corner the son of the infamous art criminal?" Emmy whispered to her cousin Vicky. Now that dinner and the first dance were over, she'd finally gotten a minute alone with the bride so she could ask about the handsome man sitting alone at a table in the back of the ballroom. She figured he must be "the one" since she'd seen him intently speed walking past a clump of photographers before they went into the church.

He'd been staring at her much of the evening.

It started when she was walking back up the aisle after the ceremony on the arm of her assigned groomsman. The intensity of his gaze had drawn her attention, but he'd looked away when she caught him staring.

And she'd *kept* catching him. His appraisal had continued throughout the toasts and as she'd tried to make conversation with the rest of the wedding party over dinner. She'd glance over at him only to find him already looking at her—enough times that he'd started grinning sheepishly, like he knew he'd been busted.

But of course if she kept catching him, it meant *she* was staring at *him* as much as he was staring at her.

It was just so hard *not* to look at him. He was tall and broad-shouldered under his impeccably tailored suit, and when he smiled as she'd catch him looking, he did it with his whole face.

"Don't look!" Emmy shriek-whispered as Vicky turned to peek over her shoulder.

"I can't tell you who he is if I can't see him," Vicky declared, not even trying to make her surveillance subtle. "Oh! Yep, that's Evan Winslow!"

"His dad even made the papers in Minnesota," Emmy said. The story of the jet-setting art dealer's fall from grace had all the makings of a Greek tragedy, and it was playing out in the tabloids. It was a true-crime story that had the nation fascinated, except instead of dead bodies there were Ponzi schemes and counterfeit art.

"Yep," said Vicky. "The trial was huge. They were one of the richest families in Miami. It's been all over the place. Poor guy. Ty says he's taken it all super hard." She cocked her head. "So you think he's cute, huh? A little nerdy for my tastes, but I dare you to go over there and talk to him."

"No way! I can't just—" Emmy's objection was cut off when the DJ cued up a horrid song that made Vicky's sorority sisters scream and rise as one.

As they swept Vicky away in a tornado of pink tulle, she

called, "Go over there. What have you got to lose? You'll never see him again anyway."

There was so much more she wanted to ask Vicky. How old was Evan Winslow? What was he studying? Vicky's new husband knew him from the University of Miami, where they were both grad students. Tyrone was doing his MBA, but she had a hard time imagining this guy in a business school. He seemed like more of an intellectual—a humanities type maybe. His hair, though currently slicked back, seemed like it was a little too long for him to fit in with the would-be capitalists, and his nerd-chic horn-rimmed glasses seemed more Buddy Holly than business. She started to make up a story. Something from the point of view of a sensitive guy forced into business school by his conniving, greedy father. The chorus could be the dad talking, but by the end of the song, the lyrics would be turned around, the guy defiantly using the father's words against him.

Well, hell. Emmy wasn't generally an assertive sort of person. She tended to hang around on the sidelines and make up little snippets of songs about what she saw unfolding around her. But Vicky was right. She was flying back to Minneapolis tomorrow, and she'd never see this guy again. In twenty-four hours, she'd be back doing battle with her parents, facing their perpetual and poorly disguised disappointment over her barista job and her "childish dreams." So why not put an end to their little mutual staring society and go say hi to the infamous Evan Winslow?

Gathering about a thousand yards of pink polyester in her arms, she hiked up her skirts and set off. He must have felt her approach, because he looked up from his cake while she was still a good twenty feet away, an expression of surprise seguing into another of those magnetic, self-deprecating grins as she got closer.

"Hey," she said, trying to make the greeting seem casual.

"Hey," he echoed. Then he added, "You're here," as if all this time he'd merely been waiting for her arrival, as if *she* had been the point of his attending the wedding.

He picked up a wedding program and slid it across the table to her.

"Ha!" She laughed in delight. If she'd been making up a story about him, it seemed he had done the same thing, in a way. Except where hers was coming together from turns of phrase and snippets of melody, his was composed of ink—garden-variety ballpoint from the look of it. He had drawn her on the back of the program, right on top of the Shakespeare sonnet that Vicky, who Emmy was pretty sure wouldn't know a sonnet if it bit her in the ass outside the context of wedding planning websites, had artfully placed on the otherwise-blank heavy-gauge paper. The funny thing was that Emmy wasn't wearing the god-awful dress in his portrait. He'd put her in shorts and a tank top, which was pretty much her uniform when she wasn't performing bridesmaid duties.

"You drew me! You're an artist?" She'd known his dad was an art dealer, but she didn't know that much about the rest of the Winslow family—she'd read the headlines but hadn't really followed the details of the trial.

He paused for long enough before answering that she started to fear she'd offended him somehow. "I used to be a painter."

"What does that mean?"

"It means I used to paint, but now I don't."

Okay then, that was clearly not a topic he was keen to discuss, so she tried another question. "Vicky said you're in grad school with Tyrone?"

"We're both at the University of Miami, but I'm doing a PhD in art history. Ty and I met in a campus running club."

Yes. The satisfying ping of having uncovered the truth in her proto-song echoed in her chest. An artist *and* an intellectual. She'd been spot-on.

"Are you from Minnesota?" he asked. "You look like you're related to Vicky."

"Yeah. She's my cousin. I'm Emmy."

He stood and stuck out his hand. "Hi, Emmy. I'm Evan."

She was on the other side of the table—too far away to reach his hand—so she walked around. Wanting to pretend that she was in control, she slowed her steps. But that was only because she wasn't entirely comfortable with the truth of the matter, which was that in her haste to reach him she'd *had* to slow her steps. She was a stupid, powerless fish he was reeling in.

He didn't let go when the handshake would normally have ended, just hitched his head toward the door. "Want to go for a walk?"

Of course she did.

* * *

"Aha!" Evan said, pushing his shoulder against the heavy metal door at the top of the stairwell. "Unlocked!" He held it for a laughing Emmy to precede him onto the roof of the banquet hall. She had her voluminous skirts gathered in one hand and her high heels dangling from the fingers of the other. "Be careful of your feet. Who knows what's up here."

She paused at the threshold and peered out. He looked over her shoulder. Yeah, the gravel that lined the ground was going to require shoes. Or…

"Eeee!" she shrieked, laughing as he swung her into his arms. "What are you doing?"

What *was* he doing? He was acting like the hero of some lame made-for-TV romantic comedy. Not his style at all. But there was something about being in limbo, teetering on the precipice between one life and another, that made every decision this evening seem less important, every action less imbued with its potential future consequences.

"If I'd known that 'go for a walk' was code for 'break onto the roof,'" she said, "I might have thought twice about accompanying you."

The roof had been the only place he could think to escape, where he could be sure there would be no photographers. But he didn't want her to feel uncomfortable, so he paused, wondering if he should turn around.

But then she craned her neck to get a better view and said, "It's gorgeous up here!"

So he crossed the roof and deposited her on some kind of ventilation structure that would do as a bench.

"Beautiful," she said, still talking about the view.

It was. The buildings of the Miami skyline he knew so well were jewels against the otherworldly pink sky of dusk. But so were the shining sapphires of her eyes.

And that was another made-for-TV thing he didn't do: compare women's eyes to gemstones. *What the hell?* There was limbo, and there was losing control of himself.

"Give me that," she said, grabbing the stolen bottle of champagne he had tucked under his arm and setting to work on the cork. When it popped, she squealed and held the fizzing bottle away from her for a moment before tipping her head back and drinking directly from it. The slanted pink light caught tendrils of blond hair escaping the pins that anchored an elaborate updo. He watched her throat undulate as she drank. Then she lifted her head, used her forearm to wipe her mouth, and grinned as she handed him the bottle, perfectly framed by the blazing sunset.

He was cursed with a painter's eye. He saw things other people didn't. He was never going to get over not painting her.

"What's your last name?" he asked, thinking, irrationally, that if he knew it, he could somehow find her later. Put a bookmark in this meeting and come back to it, even though he knew that he was going to have to draw a sharp line between what he was already starting to think of as his "old" life and whatever was going to come next.

"I'm moving to Los Angeles in two months," she said.

"So it's Emmy I'mMovingToLosAngelesInTwoMonths?" He couldn't help teasing. "That must have been a mouthful when you were a kid."

"No." She laughed. "I'm moving in two months, and I'm going to change my name when I do, I think. I haven't decided to what. So it's just Emmy for now."

Ah, so he wasn't the only one on the verge of reinventing himself. Perhaps that's why he felt this strangely, strongly compelled by her. They were of a kind. "If that's how you're going to be, I won't tell you my last name, either." She likely already knew it, but she hadn't brought it up, so he wouldn't either.

"Don't tell me," she said. "Let's just be Emmy and Evan. E and E." She took another swig of the champagne. "Like e.e. cummings."

"I will wade out till my thighs are steeped in burning flowers," he said. He wasn't sure how his brain had produced that obscure line, but he knew now how he would have painted her.

She'd been looking at the skyline, but the cummings

snippet snagged her attention, and she turned, eyes suddenly glazed with moisture.

"What's the matter?"

"I'm a songwriter," she said. "Or at least I'm trying to be."

Ah. The impending move to L.A., the name change— the pieces were coming together.

"Sometimes when I hear a line like that, it makes me despair of ever writing anything worthwhile," she said, shaking her head.

"Don't despair. You can do it."

"How do you know? You don't even know me."

He shrugged. She had intelligent eyes that looked intently at the world. That's what storytellers needed. That's probably what he had seen in her, why he had picked her out from the row of identical puffy pink dresses. "I have a feeling you're going to make it."

"You're the only one who thinks so," she whispered.

"I have a good eye," he said, struck with the urge to reassure her. "I see things other people don't." He turned so they were side by side, both facing the now rapidly darkening city —which was why he didn't have any warning when she leaned over, grabbed his cheeks, and kissed him.

Her lips were soft, and pressed so lightly against his it almost tickled. His first instinct was to push her away, because what could come of it? They were both headed for new lives, both making a break with the present.

But he couldn't make himself do it. What was so wrong with kissing a pretty girl on a rooftop? It was the perfect coda, actually, to his Miami life. So he surrendered, letting his whole body relax into the soft hunger of their kiss, forcing himself to attend to every nuance of the experience, to savor the bittersweet finale, as if he could file it away somehow, and take it out and examine it again later, like he would a memento from his past.

And, oh, he hadn't felt this alive for months. It was like she was filling him with energy he thought had been drained permanently by the police raids, the meetings with lawyers and PR people, the endless court proceedings. He sipped at her lips, letting his hands frame her face, wanting to anchor her there forever. As he deepened the kiss, testing the seam of her lips, she opened for him, but there was a tentativeness there, a hesitation.

It was like she didn't really know what she was doing.

The rogue thought entered his mind as her tongue slid along his, ripping an involuntary groan from his throat as he gently pushed her away.

"How old are you?" God, how could he have missed that? Hadn't he just been bragging about how good he was at seeing things?

Her brow furrowed. "Does it matter?" She was flushed, her pupils dilated, her breath short.

She was gorgeous.

It didn't matter how old she was, not in any elemental way. But it *did* matter here on this roof, in the clumsy corporeal world. It meant the difference between continuing this spectacular goodbye-to-his-old-life kiss and *not* continuing it.

"Tell me."

She pulled back and scooted farther away from him on the bench, confirming his fears even before she spoke. "I'm nineteen."

Right. It might be perfectly clear that this was merely a casual kiss, but he wasn't going to be *that* guy. He eyed the nearly empty champagne bottle on the ground at their feet.

That was all he needed—the story of Evan Winslow, Jr. getting a nineteen-year-old drunk and seducing her.

So much for enjoying his bittersweet Miami coda.

"How old are *you*?" she countered, a challenge in her voice.

"Twenty-six."

"That's not so bad," she said.

"Not so bad for what?" He was teasing her, but only because teasing was all he could do now. "You're right," he said. "A seven-year age difference is not bad at all for sitting on the roof talking about everything under the sun until someone notices we're gone and sends out a search party." He patted the seat beside him, shrugged out of his suit jacket, and held it out to her.

He wasn't a *total* saint, though. He liked the disappointment that washed across the striking angular face he wanted to paint so bad his fingers ached.

"Talking," she said, pouting a little but sliding back over to sit next to him and letting him slip the jacket over her shoulders.

"*Talking*," he confirmed, emphasizing the word for himself as much as for her.

"Okay, uh, what's your favorite TV show?"

"I don't really watch TV." He didn't tell her that he didn't even own one. Or that the glimpses of his family's sordid drama that he'd caught on CNN at his brother's house had been enough to reinforce his desire to never get one.

"Last concert you saw?"

He thought—hard—and came up with nothing. He had been to a few shows on the last cruise he took with his parents. His mother dragged Evan and his brother and their father on an annual luxury cruise and made them dress for dinner and generally fulfill her fantasy of the perfect Ralph Lauren family. But probably cruise ship bands playing Neil Diamond covers weren't what Emmy had in mind. "I'm not really one for live music," he finally said.

"Okaaay," she said, screwing up her face like she was trying to think of a new topic.

"It's no good," he said laughingly. "I'm completely pop-culturally illiterate."

"How come you don't paint anymore?"

Whoa. If her previous questions had been rubber-tipped darts that pinged easily off their targets, this one was a razor-sharp axe that sliced right through him.

"I don't want to talk about that," he said, which was the absolute truth, even if it didn't answer her question.

"Okay," she said, and he was surprised that she was going to accept his evasive answer. Maybe it wouldn't be so hard to upend his life after all. Maybe he could get used to being not-a-painter. "So what should we talk about?"

"You. We should talk about you." She was the most compelling person he'd met in a long time. And she was the *only* person he'd met recently who hadn't said a word about his father. "I want to know everything there is to know about you, Emmy NoLastName. Tell me about moving to L.A. Sing me a song." He turned to face her head-on. He would listen to her for as long as he could get away with it. He would listen and watch. Then he would say goodbye.

To her, and to himself.

www.ingramcontent.com/pod-product-compliance
Lightning Source LLC
Chambersburg PA
CBHW020247150626
46552CB00020B/649